T0147396

Dogman

Bob Paski

iUniverse, Inc.
New York   Bloomington

Dogman

Copyright © 2010 Bob Paski

This is a work of fiction. All of the characters, names, incidents, organizations, and dialogue in this novel are either the products of the author's imagination or are used fictitiously.

iUniverse books may be ordered through booksellers or by contacting:

iUniverse
1663 Liberty Drive
Bloomington, IN 47403
www.iuniverse.com
1-800-Authors (1-800-288-4677)

ISBN: 978-1-4502-0139-1 (pbk)
ISBN: 978-1-4502-0140-7 (ebk)

Printed in the United States of America

iUniverse rev. date: 6/24/2010

CHAPTER ONE

2:30 p.m. Thursday

The glass and steel skyline of the city loomed ahead like the citadel of an evil ruler. Overhead and beyond the buildings, the sky was a solid mass of foreboding gray clouds, swollen and seemingly ready to burst with more snow and gloom. With nothing to reflect off the polished surfaces of the structures except the pallor of another sunless winter day, the buildings were only slightly less dull in color than the sky, and the office lights that glowed from the many windows appeared to be suspended in space. The older part of the city, itself once the skyline of another time, consisted of squat, decaying buildings of brick and mortar. These structures fronted their more modern and taller brothers and made up the fortress' bulwark, no doubt holding countless dungeons and mazes.

They were growing maddeningly closer.

Allison Mayweather did not loathe the city of Lordmont. Like most life-long suburbanites, she generally found it enticing, even exhilarating, but certainly imposing. If she were going to a play at The Myth or a ball game at The Corner, she would be excited with anticipation at the prospect of viewing the denizens of the city and wondering at those who moved with intense purpose and even those who seemed to have no purpose at all. On those occasional visits to the city she would ignore the crime and pollution and the disease and indifference. She could ignore the indigence. It was not at all unpleasant from the inside of a moving vehicle.

She suspected this was not to be one of those visits. The city would be different this time.

They had shown up at her door at two o'clock in the afternoon. Lonnie and Brick and the other man. She lived in the suburb of Birchwood, northwest of Lordmont, twenty-five miles removed and affluent. There was no need for security. There was no need to expect someone other than a neighbor or friend or a delivery person to knock on your front door in the middle of the afternoon. Yet, here she was in a 2007 Lincoln Towncar heading for the city with men she didn't know. Worse yet, her daughter was sitting next to her. Did they even know about Madison before they came to her front door? Or was it a matter of unjust timing that her eleven-year-old daughter would come running and yelling into the foyer at the precise moment Brick pulled the gun from inside his coat?

Lonnie had done the talking and he was quite polite. Looking back now, though, it was obviously nothing more than perfunctory. Eloquent, clean shaven and dressed in suits beneath expensive looking overcoats, she felt a slight amount of discomfort but sensed no danger when they artfully invited themselves into the house. How quickly it had happened. Yes, she was Allison Mayweather. Yes, she was married to Frank Mayweather. No, she wasn't aware that Frank gambled. No, she wasn't aware that Frank owed a great deal of money. No, she wouldn't go with them anywhere. That was when the gun and Madison appeared simultaneously. Please don't hurt her. Please.

For twenty minutes they had been driving, now only a few miles outside of the city on the southbound Rutgers freeway, and no one had uttered a word. In that time, Allison could not bring herself to look at her abductors and only stared out the window or down at her daughter, clutching her tightly. She willed herself to stay calm, to not tremble, for fear that she might upset Madison. It seemed to Allison that Madison was quite staid, although it was generally not within her daughter to be so. Allison assumed her daughter knew there was a problem between the adults, hopefully she had no idea what, and she knew it was her place to keep her mouth shut. Allison was thankful that Madison's eleven years had not given her the experience to sense that she might be in danger. And, mercifully so, it had not given her the imagination to foresee any possibilities.

Daring to look at the men now, Allison studied their faces. They no longer possessed the persona of respectable businessmen they'd had standing outside of her front door. In her mind, they were now bigger, taller, and their facial features sharper. Their sinister nature was no longer hidden. Eyes were darker, more hooded. Nostrils flared. What she had mistaken for friendly smiles were nothing more than sneers. Even ears were longer and very close to being pointed.

The one who called himself Lonnie sat in the front seat on the passenger side. Black hair, slicked straight back with some sort of grease, and pale blue eyes set against skin that was a sickly pale made him appear as if he were a creature of the night. The driver was the man called Brick – the one who had brandished the weapon. He was the shortest of the three but he was built sturdy. He sported a beard and mustache but the top of his head had been shaved clean and the skin there, perhaps one shade lighter than the color of coal, reflected even the slightest hint of light. The other man, the man whose name Allison did not yet know, was the scariest of the three. Back at her front door, Lonnie hadn't bothered to introduce him and he stood apart from the other two. She felt then that it was almost as if they were ignoring him, as if they would have preferred he wasn't there. While Lonnie and Brick were clearly dangerous, she perceived in their eyes a level of common sense that would rein in their menace. She could perceive no such thing in this man's eyes. They were a lifeless brown, the color of coffee after two hits of cream. His cheeks were ruddy and scarred, having been ravaged by the teen years. His hair, the same dull color that matched his eyes, was receding but he tried to hide the fact by combing it over from the left side. And he was huge.

The man glanced over and caught her gazing at him. She turned away quickly but not before he gave her a smile that dripped of such lecherousness that instantly a shudder ran through her body. The shock of that look from a stranger who now controlled her movement was absolute. She was not in Birchwood anymore and she knew, even though only twenty miles or so intervened between her and her three-thousand square-foot home with the diligently manicured and watered lawn, the degree of separation from the comfort and innocence of her life could not be computed using linear measurement. The sudden spasm caused Madison to look up at her. Allison attempted a comforting smile but found it difficult to accomplish through the tears that began welling in her eyes. Her daughter sensed the change and huddled closer to her mother. Allison responded with a tighter hug and gazed out the window at the office lights that now refracted outward from their center.

Allison was not a religious person. Some called her devout simply because of her weekly sojourns to the First Presbyterian Church of Birchwood. She saw it as a responsibility to the community, to her husband's work, and to her daughter's upbringing. Only she and her God knew the truth. She began to pray anyway.

Carson, the man whose name Allison had yet to learn, continued to smile when he saw the fear manifest in her eyes. He'd seen that look before and it never failed to exhilarate him, never failed to give him a feeling of power. Holding someone's fate in your own hands was an aphrodisiac like no other.

Five people in the car had caused the temperature in the small space to rise significantly and Carson watched as she loosened her winter coat. This enhanced the view down the front of her dress and drew his eyes like a magnet. Not only the heat but her fright, as well, caused the slightest glistening of perspiration to form across her chest. He watched a bead of sweat course its way down between the modest swellings and disappear beneath the cloth of her dress and wished to lick the salty tear from her skin. He was surprised that she chose to wear a light dress in the dead of winter but it pleased him. The material hugged her physique. His gaze slowly lowered and hovered briefly at the bunching of the cloth at her crotch and then continued downward to the hem of her dress. There, creamy porcelain skin covered muscular, but oh so thoroughly, feminine thighs and the stirrings that had only just begun quickly became a full-blooded alert. In no way conspicuous, Carson shifted in his seat.

His gaze returned to her breasts and he envisioned their warmth in his hand and mouth. They appeared perfect beneath the dress. He hated large breasts. They were sloppy and cool to the touch. They were nothing but overly large glands, too far removed from the pulsing arteries that circulated a woman's heat and her ardor. And when he was raping a woman, despite her disgust, her blood pulsed faster and her warmth grew. It was a complete turn off to feel large protrusions of flabby and cool skin shaking and vibrating beneath him.

Carson wondered when he would get his chance. They had never used a client's family members as collateral before. This was new territory, so he wasn't sure of the routine. He assumed he'd get the chance to watch her alone at some point, but he doubted Gerard would give him the go ahead to do what he pleased with her. At least, he hoped, until they were certain the loser wasn't going to pay. He only knew that she wasn't to be harmed in any way while it played out. He had made a mistake once before when they were holding a client. He'd been without a little finger on his right hand ever since. To this day, in his small mind, he didn't understand why Gerard went so ballistic. Afterall, he had left the guy alive and mobile.

Carson glanced down at where the finger used to be. The finger he could do without but the pain wasn't something he needed to experience again. Gerard tolerated no indiscretions when it came to collecting money. Rules were rules and he was a man of his word. Carson's only hope was that Mayweather couldn't come up with the money. If the fool couldn't do it within forty-eight hours, then Gerard might let him have his way with her. Come on Mayweather, he thought to himself, help me out here. And with that, he let out an audible snort.

Allison glanced over at Carson when she heard him make a noise. He looked up at her and smiled again. Maybe he'd do the mother, too, when he was done with the girl.

Allison heard the click of the turn signal and felt the car begin to slow. Fighting through her apprehension, she thought it wise to pay attention to the route the Towncar was taking in case she needed to recite it later. Exiting the freeway, the vehicle turned left onto Lafayette

Street heading east. The four-lane avenue was on the outer perimeter of Lordmont and, in this area of the city, most of the structures were still occupied by the tail end of the suburban migration. Single family homes, run down by years of use and vandalism, were interspersed with ongoing, but struggling, businesses. Dry cleaners, bars and thrift shops, at one time a benefit to the neighborhood, struggled to hang on, barely able to succeed now because of the declining economic stability of their neighbors. Windows protected by iron bars were the vogue. Four blocks later, the car turned south again and headed deeper into the city on Grant Avenue. Slowly, houses became scarce, and were replaced by tenements. The buildings grew larger and the architecture more ornate, stylish in an earlier time, but now out of date. They also grew more vacant. Iron bars were still popular but there were fewer windows for them to protect. They passed a school that had been named in honor of someone called P.S. 120 and, to Allison, it looked as if the school should have been unused except that lights shone from every window. She glanced around at the surrounding neighborhood and wondered sadly where all of those children lived. No one was on the streets and, if not for the lights in windows, the area would have appeared uninhabited.

The vehicle turned right onto a street that might have been named Jamison but she couldn't be certain because the sign had been spray painted red. Another quick left and two more rights and she lost any hope of leading anyone anywhere. She looked for some sort of landmark, or, perhaps a beacon, but it all looked the same. Brownstone structure after brownstone structure, some still intact, others with collapsed walls, their jagged edges reaching upward, appearing to be relics from a world war, left her slightly dizzy. Through the light snow that was feathering its way downward she could see that the heart of the city was closer. She glimpsed Angel Heights Tower between two five-story apartment buildings but was not close enough to use it as a point of reference. After ten minutes or so and several turns, the Towncar pulled up to the curb in front of a three-story building.

Lonnie turned to the back seat. "Watch them. We'll be right back." He gazed at Carson for a few moments making certain his statement registered with the man.

The two men in the front seat exited the car and walked up the two steps to an entry door. Allison watched them as they went. The steel door had been painted black but was marred and streaked sporadically with orange and blue paint. After the two men disappeared, she looked above the entryway and saw what remained of a sign. The name of whoever had owned the building or company that was once housed inside began with the letter 'W'. That was all that remained on the left side of the sign. On the far right side she could make out the word 'Storage'. The four wide windows on the first story, two on either side of the entrance, and the six across the second level were covered with plywood. Above that, her view was blocked by the roof of the car. She chose not to crane her neck to see the third story for fear that any movement she might make would cause some kind of reaction from Carson.

After a few minutes of waiting in the idling vehicle that had become stifling, and not knowing when the two men might return, she cautiously spoke. "May we get out and stretch our legs? It's awfully cramped in here. And hot, too."

Carson gazed over at her, pondering her question. After a time, he responded, "Okay, but don't do nothin' stupid."

Allison opened the door on her side of the car and started to pull Madison with her. "Come on, honey, let's stand outside for a little while."

Carson grabbed Madison by the arm. "She'll get out on this side."

"It's okay, honey. Go ahead." Allison prayed he wouldn't hurt her and would have voiced it if she didn't think it would have scared her daughter half to death.

The snow fell harder now, no longer simply drifting to the ground. The ankle-high beige suede boots she managed to grab before they forced her out of her house were more about form than function. They were warm and stylish enough but not truly made for snow. She slipped in the slush and, if not for the arm rest on the inside of the back door, which she had to grasp quite suddenly, the back of her deep-brown, wool slacks would have been covered with snow. She made her way carefully around the back of the car, placing her hand on the trunk for balance, and stood next to her daughter. Carson maintained his grip on the girl's arm and the three of them silently watched the increasingly heavy snowfall.

Fifty yards ahead of the car a woman in a heavy coat and several scarves that covered her head and face was making her way toward them on the sidewalk. She was carrying a large bag made of some sort of cloth material. She would stop every so often, bend down and inspect something beneath the snow and then move on. The three of them watched the woman but, after a moment, Allison remembered that she had wanted to see beyond the second floor. The windows of the third floor were not boarded, nor were they broken. Light shone from the far southside window. Nothing about the building was remarkable. It was simply a square building of reddish sandstone brick, lacking any of the architectural design that had marked its era.

As her gaze strayed along the building's upper floor toward the north, movement in the lower corner of her eye caught her attention. She glanced down and saw a man peeking beyond the corner of the building. He stood in the ten-foot wide alleyway that separated the building that Allison was now in front of from an identical structure. His clothes were shabby. He wore a long dark woolen coat whose hem, if it would have had one, would have reached halfway down his shins. Instead tattered shreds of the coat licked the ground. The stocking cap that covered his head was probably bright red when it was new, but it wasn't bright anymore and was stained with something brown. The man's gaze continually shifted between Allison and Carson, and she thought she saw him smile.

Carson watched the woman come closer and sneered at her. He hated street people. Most of them kept to themselves but those that didn't were just a pain in his ass. They were relentless beggars and, for a reason he could never comprehend, overly nosy. A smile crossed his face remembering all those he had abused. Carson played with these people like he was a cat and they were mice. He never quite killed them but played with them until they were bloodied and barely capable of moving. When he was done with them most died slow, lonely, agonizing deaths in some abandoned building. The woman was approaching the front entrance and Carson glanced up at the third floor wondering where his two cohorts were. If they didn't come back real soon he was going to have to scare off the woman. Not that she was anyone with which to be concerned. He just liked doing it.

Not wanting to wait any longer, Carson looked over at Allison and her daughter. "Stay here. You move and I'll hurt ya'." He walked toward the woman.

When Carson was out of earshot, Madison, with a tremble in her voice, said, "Mom, why did he say he would hurt us?"

At the same time as her daughter spoke, Allison heard a sound from the corner of the building. She looked over at the man who was still standing there and he was now motioning to her.

"Come on," the man said in a hoarse whisper. "Come on. Now." He began motioning more quickly.

Madison heard the whisper, too, and turned toward the sound. She looked up at her mother and moved closer to her, not knowing what to think of the creepy man hiding by the building. Allison looked from Carson to the man and back again. She had no clue what to make of the situation. Carson was almost to the woman.

"You have to come now," the man whispered again.

Somewhere near the steps Carson had found a two by four plank and had picked it up. He was starting to wave it menacingly toward the woman. The man by the corner kept motioning to Allison. It seemed to her that the man wanted her to follow. Why, she wondered. Did he somehow know why she was here? How could he? Frank wouldn't let her stay here very long. Her feet were getting cold and she could feel Madison shaking. They would be warm soon, once Lonnie and Brick came back and took them inside. The man at the corner was most assuredly homeless. What could he possibly offer them? And why? Did he mean to help them? She saw Carson raise the piece of wood high over his head.

"Hey, ya' old bitch. What the fuck are ya' doin' 'round here?" he yelled at her.

Startled, the woman stopped in her tracks and stared at the large man, seemingly unaware that she had crossed some line.

Allison was unprepared to make this kind of decision. Her life had not trained her for it. Unable to see past the current moment, she was incapable of putting the alternatives side by side and evaluating them. Her common sense, unworldly as it was, told her to stay put. She hadn't led the type of life that would put her in harm's way, at least not the type of harm she envisioned Carson seemed capable of inflicting.

She watched Carson close in on the woman. She remembered the lecherous look in his eyes and the way he stared at Madison. Hungrily. She knew she had to get away from him. She didn't have any idea what she might be plunging headlong into but if it was away from Carson, it had to be better. Didn't it? She froze with indecision. The man at the corner still motioned. Carson yelled louder at the woman.

"Mom, I think he's going to hurt her. Why?" The girl drew even closer to her mother.

That was enough for her.

"God help me," she said softly but aloud. She looked down at Madison, grabbed her hand and said to her, "Come on, run." To Allison's surprise, her daughter obeyed with no hesitation.

As they ran toward the corner, the man turned and ran down the alley ahead of them. Just as they skirted the corner, Allison heard someone yell, "Hey!"

CHAPTER TWO

2:57 p.m. Thursday

In the alley, Allison was running in soundless slow motion. Immediately after she heard someone yell from the front of the building, all audio stimulation had cut off. The heavy snowfall helped to deaden the sound of their footfalls in the alley but it was the myriad thoughts assaulting her brain that caused her ears to malfunction. Her imagination was in high gear and she was close to cerebral overload. Barely ten yards into the alley and the shabbily dressed man, into whose hands she had just put her and Madison's lives, disappeared around a corner of the building to the right. It was only twenty yards ahead but it seemed miles. She glanced down at Madison, assuming the girl was slowing her down, only to find that she was the one lagging. She tried to pump her legs harder but she felt as if she were in a dream. Finally, the corner arrived and they negotiated the turn with little slipping. She saw her daughter's snow covered leather Adidas as they turned and managed to worry about frostbitten little toes. When she looked up they were in another narrow corridor with the building to the right and a ten-foot high wooden fence to the left. The man was gone.

"Where is he?" Allison said aloud.

"I don't know," Madison responded.

Allison's hearing was still good enough to notice the quiver in her daughter's voice. What am I doing, she screamed to herself. They were underdressed in freezing weather, her daughter was near tears, their shoes were wet and cold, and they were running somewhere after, what appeared to be, a homeless man, whom she had recklessly presumed was going to lead them to safety.

"This is crazy!" she yelled. She began to slow down.

"Keep going!" Madison screamed at her.

Startled, Allison picked up her pace again. Unable to make her own decisions, why not let your eleven year-old make them for you, she thought. After all, this was already stupid. Up ahead of them, two large black plastic garbage bins on rollers allowed about two feet of passage. Allison let Madison go through first, not letting go of her hand. Just as she was passing between the bins and the back wall of the building she heard a loud crack that echoed off the brick of the surrounding structures. The sound was so startling that she lost her footing and Madison's hand.

She didn't want to think about what the sound might have been, although she had a good idea. Fleetingly, she realized what little justice television did to the sound. Instead she concentrated on getting to her feet. The area around the bins had been heavily trod on recently. The ridges formed by the boot prints had frozen unevenly and had become slippery. As she tried to scramble to her feet, she saw Madison being yanked away from her to the left. A moment later, a hand inside a woolen knit glove, except for where the index and middle finger poked through, grabbed her hand and pulled her crawling through a hole in the wooden fence.

When Brick opened the front door of the old warehouse it sucked in a flurry of the heavy snow that pelted his face.

"Jesus," he muttered, wiping a hand across his face and over the top of his smooth, dark head. Just off the steps to the right he saw Carson readying to level a blow at the old woman. He immediately stepped out onto the stoop looking left just as Allison's dark brown pant leg was disappearing beyond the building.

"Hey!" he yelled.

He leapt down the two steps trying to turn to his left as he landed. The leather Gino Cheruitti shoes from Acapulco, so sleek and fashionable when he first purchased them but now just reasonably cheap and creased, were not made for winter. His feet went out from under him, landing him hard on the sidewalk. He was up quickly, though, and made for the alley. The downward swath of the board that Carson held ceased at the sound of Brick's voice. Seeing what was happening, he began running in Brick's direction, worrying about the pain of losing another finger. If he had to lose a finger again, he hoped it would be his left pinky. The old woman with the bag, being pardoned from her beating, scurried away as best she could in the other direction. Just as Carson was passing the steps, Lonnie came out of the building and began moving with them.

In the alley between the buildings Brick was greeted with pretty much the same view of Allison as he had just moments before. He headed for the far end and pulled out his revolver as he went. He fired a round into the air hoping it might persuade mother and daughter to abort their attempt at escape.

From behind him Lonnie yelled, "Stop it, you asshole! You wanna draw attention to this?"

Brick skidded to a stop at the end of the alley and Carson and Lonnie just averted plowing into him. When they looked down the adjacent alleyway there was no sign of them, except for the tracks left in the deepening snow.

When they made it to the garbage bins they saw the matted and trampled snow just beyond them. The disorder in the snow went to the left and stopped abruptly at the foot of the fence. Shallow tracks, tracks almost completely covered now, led further down the alley. Lonnie studied the tracks for a moment, then moved to the fence, placed his shoe against it and shoved. Four planks, two feet wide in all, moved outward against the pressure.

"Through here," he said at Carson and motioned for him to go through first.

On the other side was a small area behind yet another building, although this was of cinder block and only one story. Long untended grass and weeds poked up through the snow and numerous small mounds indicated piles of trash that had been strewn around the yard. Several old tires, without their wheel hubs, had been leaned against the back of the building. Three sets of tracks led to an opening in the back wall.

The door that used to seal the opening lay on the cement floor three feet inside. Wet tracks with small piles of yet to be melted snow about them lead off to the left through another entryway. Off to the right was a small room that appeared as if it might have been an office at one time. On an adjacent wall was another doorway. The late afternoon illumination, hampered by the snowfall, was fading fast. The inside of the building held little light.

Lonnie looked over at Carson. "Go back to the Lincoln and get the flashlights out of the trunk."

"They couldn't have gotten far. Let's find 'em now. We got enough light." His fingers were twitching.

"If they're here, Brick and I'll find them. If they got out of this building were going to need flashlights to spot their tracks. Now go,"

After Carson left, Lonnie said to Brick, "How the fuck did they know about that hole in the fence? Go that way."

"The tracks go that way, man."

"Yeah, but I don't know where any of the rooms go, do you? They could be anywhere."

Don't upset the man anymore than he already is, Brick thought to himself. Arguing with Gerard's right hand man is like arguing with the man himself. He moved off to the right into the small office, shaking his head after Lonnie was out of sight. Why Gerard put so much faith in Lonnie was beyond comprehension. The guy couldn't be trusted. Why couldn't Gerard see that? As his eyes slowly adjusted to the dimness in the small room, he could see that there was nothing but a small folding chair and table. Some old papers that had some sort of printing on them that he couldn't make out were spread across the table and floor. He noticed a light switch on the wall next to the door he had just come through and couldn't imagine that electricity still flowed through the building. He tried it anyway and the room remained dark. He opened the door on the adjacent wall and saw nothing but blackness.

"Jesus Christ. Aren't there any windows in this place?" He slid cautiously across the floor with his hands out in front of him.

Lonnie followed the tracks through the entryway to the left and what little light there was revealed to him a makeshift garage. Along the side wall was a long wooden shelf that still held old and rusted oil cans, filthy rags and small tools here and there. In the middle of the floor he saw two small ramps, the kind do-it-yourselfers use to change the oil in their cars in their own driveway. He didn't see the third heavy, metal ramp right in front of him and drove his shin into it with his next step. He let out an expletive, rubbed his shin and stepped around it. His steps became shorter and more wary. As his eyes became accustomed to the lack of light, he could still make out wet tracks that led on ahead. Pale light outlined a large opening on the wall in front of him and it took him a moment before he realized that it was a garage door. When he reached it, he felt for and found a handle but it wouldn't budge. He then moved toward the inner wall and found another door. It opened into more blackness but the space didn't seem to be deserted. He heard shuffling not more than ten feet from him and it was coming closer. With practiced quickness, he pulled his weapon from the holster inside his coat and pointed it out in front of him ready to shoot into the void. Lonnie was not one to panic easily but hearing shuffling coming toward him in complete and total darkness was unsettling even to him. The hair on the back of his neck stood up and he backed up a couple of paces, his eyes searching. The scraping sounds continued to move closer. He gripped the gun a little tighter, his finger feathering the trigger.

"Damn," Brick muttered from within the darkness.

Lonnie let out a long breath and holstered his gun. "Nothin', huh?"

"What! Oh, Jesus, man, you scared me. Where the hell are you? I can't see a thing in here."

Lonnie snickered briefly. "You can't see my white ass? I bet if you smile I could see you."

"Very funny." He would normally laugh at Lonnie's wisecracks about their skin tone differences but he was just plain scared of the dark. Not that anyone would ever know the extent of his fear. And if they did, he'd have to kill them.

Moments later they saw the beam of a flashlight pierce the darkness in the garage. Carson found the two men, joined them and gave them each a flashlight. They surveyed the floor about them and found the tracks. As nightfall neared, the temperature was dropping fast and the snow and wetness of the footprints was now beginning to freeze where it lay. The tracks guided them back into the area where Lonnie and Brick had met in the darkness and then disappeared down some stairs that led to a basement.

"Let's go down," Lonnie commanded.

Both of the other men hesitated and looked at him.

"What? What are you waiting for?"

Brick said timidly, "Rats." Another fear manifesting itself.

Lonnie snorted, "Rats? You know how fucking cold it is in here? It's hardly ten degrees above zero. Besides, there's probably no garbage down there, anyway." When the other two still hesitated, he shook his head in disgust. "Jesus Christ, I'll go first then." With a great deal of sarcasm, he added, "I'll fend them off."

Lonnie led them down the short flight of stairs. It wasn't without some reluctance. He shared their fear of the rat. What you could see of the floor was dirt, and the walls were nothing but poured concrete. The height of the cellar was no more than five feet and they had to stoop as they moved around. There was refuse everywhere but it wasn't the kind to attract rodents. More old tools, broken furniture and scraps of wood and glass were strewn about the area. It consisted of only one room and it wasn't large. There was no sign of the women. After a few moments of searching the area, a creaking noise caused all three flashlight beams to focus on one of the corners at the front of the building. Just above the poured concrete and below the joists supporting the floor above was a boarded up window. From their vantage point they could plainly see the hinges on the left side of the plywood board. They could also see the wood moving slightly in response to the small gusts of wind that buffeted it from the outside. A metal folding chair sat directly beneath it. Brick walked over to the window and swung it open, revealing the almost imperceptible light that existed at four o'clock on an overcast midwinter afternoon.

Somehow she managed to operate on a physical level, putting one foot in front of the other, maintaining her forward momentum. She could feel the cold and focus on her surroundings. On an intellectual and emotional level, functioning properly was nearly impossible. One hour from now, she probably wouldn't even remember this moment. Through it all, motherly instincts remained intact. When they had first entered the abandoned garage, the man took hold of Madison's hand to lead them through. Fearing that he would run off with her, Allison silently but insistently inserted herself between them. Later, when they climbed through the window of the basement she found herself absurdly pleased with the man when he helped Madison through first and then her, so that her daughter and the man would not be alone either inside or out.

Allison was relieved to be out of the garage. The feeling of holding a stranger's hand in the near total darkness of the abandoned building was something she couldn't describe. She almost allowed herself a smile realizing the irony of this feeling of comfort now that she was outside. Such was the theory of relativity as it applied to emotions.

The neighborhood they faced as they exited the building seemed to be the beginning of a residential district. Although the side of the street on which the garage stood was littered with the remnants of structures that at one time held small businesses, across the street were ten identical three-story town homes. As they hurriedly crossed the street, Allison noted that only four of the homes, the two on either end of the block, had lights coming from their windows. Four others were simply dark, while the two middle structures were scarred by fire. In the upper two floors of each, all windows were completely gone and the openings were tinged with black. On the bottom floors the windows were merely broken and in one she saw a ragged set of drapes.

On the snow covered, broken, and ankle sprain-inducing sidewalk fronting the burned out homes Allison decided it was time to find out what the man's intentions were. They were moving at just less than a dead run and speaking was difficult through heavy breaths.

"Where are you taking us?" she panted. The amount and thickness of the steam that escaped her mouth as she spoke surprised her.

"Somewhere safe." He looked back but not at her, only over her shoulder toward the garage.

"I've got to get my daughter warm, now."

"Very soon. We've got to keep moving."

"I'm okay, Mom," Madison said. She, too, didn't bother to look at her mother and just kept running.

"Your feet must be freezing, honey. I know mine are."

The girl was insistent. "Mom, I'm okay."

She wanted to stop but couldn't. She glanced back over her shoulder and saw no one in pursuit but knew they couldn't be far behind. She wanted to pick up Madison to take her feet from the snow but knew that would only slow them down. She wanted to scream at what was happening to her but knew it would only help her pursuers. She wanted to scream at the man they were following, a man who hadn't said more than ten words since they started and never, it seemed, more than two at a time, but knew that wouldn't be productive either. So she kept running and spoke only because she needed to. "This is nuts!"

As they were passing the second of the two burnt-out homes, a several-years old, rust-eaten station wagon stopped at the curb three houses down. Bundled in heavy winter clothing, two small children bolted from the passenger side and ran toward one of the town homes. An adult female emerged from the driver's side and immediately noticed the three people running along the sidewalk. Allison could not see the woman's face clearly but she knew the woman was watching them. How odd this must appear to her, Allison thought. For a brief moment she considered calling out to the woman, asking for her help, but could not do it. Overriding motherly instincts wouldn't let her endanger the woman or her children. Instead, perhaps a cry for help to another mother, or perhaps just to be seen by someone else, Allison kept her face toward the woman, even as they turned up the driveway of one of the abandoned homes two lots away from the station wagon.

They entered the home on the east through a side door, held hands through the darkened kitchen, living room and dining room and exited on the south side through what used to be beautifully sculpted French doors, now pitifully marred and holding window panes of jagged glass.

They ran across the backyard, went through a hole in the rusted chain link fence and ran across another back yard.

For the next forty-five minutes Allison and Madison followed the man. Their pace slowed due to endurance and the deepening snow but remained steady. The pattern of their venture seemed haphazard, at first, but after awhile Allison noticed a consistency to it. In and out of old homes and buildings, sometimes exiting on the same floor, sometimes exiting out of a basement, running through backyards and garages, but never staying on the street for very long. Allison had to admit that she saw a certain ingenuity to it. In one particularly cunning move, although at the time she feared its danger, they had entered an old hardware store and exited through a bathroom window using a ten foot long two by twelve board from the storeroom directly into the building next door only six feet away. Once through, the man had pulled the plank through into the building in which they stood.

Through it all the snow kept falling and the temperature inched downward. Finally, when Allison was just about too tired to go on any further and worried that they were getting dangerously close to being in the cold too long, the man stopped. They were standing at the back edge of a narrow vacant lot in between two brick structures. The structure on the far side of the lot, thirty feet away, was a bar that, from what Allison could tell, was still in operation. A homemade sign on the facing wall of the building declared it was Sam's Bar. She could see a neon sign protruding out over the sidewalk in the front that was attempting to say the same thing but only the 'S' still had life. Across the road from where they stood, cheaply constructed clapboard houses lined the street. Allison thought this neighborhood appeared different than what she had been seeing for the last several minutes but couldn't put her finger on it immediately. As she gazed up and down the block, lights glowed from less than half of the homes. After a moment, she realized that there were large, stately oak trees in the front yards of each of the houses. Her addled but recovering mind wouldn't let her remember seeing any trees before this. In another time, the heavy snow falling quietly on this avenue might have been pleasing to the eye but the age and deterioration of the clapboards couldn't be denied, even at nightfall. The few cars parked here and there didn't look as if they were capable of mobility. Except for the snow, this place, too, was without movement. Sadly, she considered it desolate.

"Over here," the man said.

They followed him behind the building closest to them. Leaning against the wall was an old wheelbarrow, though it might be considered only a barrow since it was only capable of being dragged. Behind it was a sheet of plywood that appeared to be securely fastened to the wall above the cinder block foundation. On either side of the board were two smaller pieces secured by screws. He turned both pieces and the board came loose, revealing an opening in the brick. He climbed through legs first and extended his hands back out to help them.

Once Allison and Madison climbed down off the wooden crate, which had been placed directly below the opening on the inside of the building, the man replaced the board, securing it again with two similar pieces of wood on the opposite side. With the lateness of the day and no windows, they were completely engulfed in darkness. The women stood silently while the man made rustling noises ten feet away. Now closed in with this strange man and having no idea what was to come next, Allison moved her daughter behind her as she faced the direction of the sounds and felt for one of the small wooden pieces on the board that led to the outside. They stood there for what seemed like minutes, Allison frantically searching the blackness for whatever was coming. It grew completely silent for several seconds and Allison's fear was beginning to overtake her.

"Mom, what's he doing?"

Instead of the nervous quiver she had heard in her daughter's voice before, she now heard fright. Allison doubted her sanity, once again, for what she had gotten them into. At the same time, the protector in her took over. She turned one of the handles on the board and reached for the other.

"Get on the box, Madison. We're getting out of here," she whispered.

Just then the beam of a flashlight appeared and the man came toward them carrying candles, wool blankets and a knapsack. When he neared them he saw Madison standing on the box and Allison's hand on the second wooden handle. The faint ambient light given off by the flashlight did not allow her to see his face clearly but it was enough to see that his eyes were a deep shade of brown. It was also enough for her to see them change. She didn't know this man but the dispirit that appeared in his eyes was unmistakable.

Quietly he said, "You're safe with me."

He walked past them and Allison could see the light pass over cinder block walls and empty shelves. He moved toward the opposite wall and lit three candles, which he placed in a triangle about six feet apart. He spread a blanket on the floor, threw another on top of it and then laid a third blanket on the floor as far from the others as he could while still remaining within the triangle of candles.

"It's warmer over here. Some heat comes through the door at the top of the stairs." He sat down on the farthest blanket and started pawing through the knapsack.

Allison took her daughter's hand and led her over to the blankets. After they sat down, the man produced a box of *Saltine* crackers. He pulled a brown cellophane package from the carton and Allison noted that half of the column of crackers was gone but the opened end had been folded neatly in an attempt to lock in the freshness. He held them out in offer. Madison reached for them but Allison took them first. She opened the package and removed a cracker. Warily, she brought it to her lips, discreetly trying to catch the scent of anything foul. They were stale but edible and she handed the package to her daughter.

"I know you're hungry but go easy," Allison commanded, "They're going to make you thirsty and we don't have anything to drink."

On cue, the man pulled a clear plastic bottle from the knapsack. The label had long ago worn away but she recognized it as a bottle that at one time held *Evian* water. She doubted that the original water was still inside.

"Please don't worry, it's okay, too," the man said gazing at Allison, "Sorry, it's all that's here."

It was distinctly warmer. Certainly not the comfort level of her living room, but not unbearable. She was actually starting to feel uncomfortable underneath the heavy wool blanket with her winter coat still covering her. She remembered that Madison still wore wet shoes.

"Honey, take off your shoes and socks and lay them out by the candles. Maybe they'll dry out some. Then wrap your feet up inside the blanket." As she helped her daughter remove wet knee-length socks, Madison's bare legs reminded Allison of how many times she had scolded her daughter for not dressing properly. "Madison, why were you out in the snow wearing a dress? Why do I have to constantly tell you…"

"Mom," Madison pleaded, nodding her head toward the man.

Allison shook her head in exasperation but let it go. She gazed around the basement taking in their surroundings. She had no idea what was on the floor above or why there was some heat finding its way below but she was too thankful to care. For the most part, the basement was dry. She could see small puddles here and there mostly near the wall where they had entered but there were none close to where the blankets lay. Metal shelving units lined one wall and two more jutted out into the middle of the room. They held nothing but dust. Several more wooden crates like the one they had climbed on were scattered about. They, too, were empty. Finally, she looked back at the man. He had taken off his stocking cap and his dark brown hair, like his beard, was surprisingly short but severely uneven. It was the chic look of self-barbering with only a pair of shears and no mirror. The flannel shirt and jeans he wore underneath his ragged overcoat were in better condition but still in need of serious mending. He sat cross-legged staring at one of the candles. The awkwardness was growing by leaps and bounds.

"So," Allison said. He looked up at her. "Who are you and what do you want with us?"

At the time Lonnie, Brick and Carson began to follow the tracks away from the garage, they were still quite discernible. They even managed to get through the town home and out the back through the French doors. Before they got to the fence at the back of the property, the heavy snow was quickly making the tracks difficult to see.

"Son of a bitch," Lonnie breathed, "There's no fucking way we're going to be able to follow them in this snow." He turned to Carson and directed the flashlight beam into his eyes. "What the hell were you thinking about?"

"I didn't think they'd run. Where were they gonna go?" He looked down at the snow considering the stupidity of his statement. Obviously, they were going somewhere.

"Well, they're sure as hell going somewhere now, aren't they?"

"Look," Brick interjected, "I'm certainly not going to defend the fool but he's got a point. Where were they supposed to go? For the most part, this place is a ghost town. How are a woman and a girl from the suburbs supposed to find their way around down here? No way. But they found that hole in that fence and they found their way through that garage with hardly any light. I mean, down the basement and out a window?" He paused momentarily and nodded toward the town home. "And they found their way through this house, too. It's like they know where they're going. I don't know how. It's as if somebody's leading them."

"Who could they possibly know down here?" Lonnie sneered, "And if they did know somebody, how would they know where they were going to be? And how would this somebody know their way around like this? It just doesn't make any sense. I think they're just lucky so far."

"Could be," Brick admitted without much conviction.

Carson was silently looking at the snow thinking about his fingers.

"Well, we gotta go tell Gerard what happened. Carson, you and I'll go see him. Brick, you get the word on the street who we're looking for. And then start looking yourself. Once Gerard's done with us, we'll start looking."

CHAPTER THREE

3:31 p.m. Thursday

The lock of the century. That's what Jimmy had called it. And Jimmy hadn't been wrong before. Every two years or so he called Frank with another lock of the century and every time Frank laid the bet. Without fail, each bet was a winner. And every time Frank escalated the wager. Whether it was the point spread of a major football game or the odds on a boxing spectacle, Jimmy was right on. How many times had his team been behind only to dominate the second half and prove Jimmy right once again? Several years ago, during a phone call at three in the morning, which seemed to be the hour of Jimmy's inspirations, Frank had asked him why the locks were never on other sports. Football and boxing were wars, he had said. They didn't take place daily and every one of them counted. The participants got in each other's faces. The combat was so close that the skin and blood and breath of the opponents melded. The fundamentals of each sport were acts of man's most base nature. Hit your opponent as hard as you possibly can as many times as you could get away with. It was these kinds of acts that made the game true in spite of the referee's blunders. The other major sports had seasons that lasted too long and games that were played too frequently, allowing the participants to lose their edge to boredom. Baseball players rarely saw contact and opponents were too far away to become personal enemies. Basketball was played in underwear and, thanks to Magic, Larry and Michael, had become nothing more than high-speed choreography. Hockey was closer but the goons were a thing of the past and the scoring was just too low.

The AFC teams hadn't mounted any kind of threat to the NFC teams over the course of the season. Why would the Super Bowl be any different? Green Bay had cruised through the season with only two losses early on. After the fifth week they didn't just beat their opponent every Sunday, they annihilated them. The Pack was back and every bit as strong as the teams of the Sixties. The Tennessee Titans, a Cinderella team only a year ago with a brand new quarterback only one year removed from college, also eased through their season with only three losses but they mostly played the weak sisters of the AFC, where speed and deception were the call to arms. The spread was eight and Jimmy laughed at the losses the books would take. Lay the bet early, Jimmy had said, before the spread widened. Frank obeyed, and his faith in Jimmy helped him ignore the fact that the spread actually tightened to six by game time.

Jimmy was a wise man when it came to odds making and over the years he had shared a good deal of information about the art with Frank. What Jimmy neglected to tell him, and did so because it was the number one credo of all successful gamblers and generally not in need of repeating, was never bet more than you could afford to lose. But Frank was not a successful gambler. In between locks from Jimmy he lost much more than he won and he had stopped keeping track long ago. Allison's father's law firm was paying him undeservedly well and he had yet to begin to feel the pinch of his burdensome habit. Despite the more than adequate compensation he received, he wanted more. He wanted enough to break free of the daily grind and live at a more leisurely pace. When Jimmy called, and he had been waiting, Frank had decided it was time to separate himself from the pack.

A half million would do it. He didn't have it, hell, he didn't even have half that amount liquid. But why should he worry, Jimmy hadn't let him down yet. When he won, he could put that together with the two hundred grand or so he had stashed and make some mighty tasty investments.

When the Titan's young quarterback put the ball in the air with only two ticks left on the clock, realization hit him so hard that he nearly vomited onto the Berber carpet in his living room. As the ball spiraled toward the end zone, the Packers were already celebrating with an eleven point lead, and any defense they attempted was only half hearted. The announcers barely remarked on the Titan's touchdown, singing the praises of the warriors from Green Bay, all the while knowing the havoc the touchdown was creating in Vegas.

Thirty minutes ago Frank Mayweather had begun pacing the plush hunter-green carpet of his office in downtown Birchwood. He was unable to stop. With each long pace from his lanky six-foot frame he gently kicked the putter he held in his right hand. For the most part, Frank Mayweather was a good man, a typically normal man. Admittedly, he was only a fair attorney but he worked hard and cared about his clients. He had never been a star burning brightly at the law firm but he plodded along, got his work done and brought in just enough new business not to be a burden to the partners. Just enough not to be a total disappointment to Allison's father. Like many men, though, men in their late thirties with forty fast approaching and life slipping by faster with each passing day, he wanted a change. The half million would have done it.

He stopped his pacing, picked up the telephone from his desk and called home for the fourth time in the last half an hour. He believed Lonnie had them but in his heart he hoped he'd been lying. When Allison's voice, once again, came on the recorder after five rings, Frank succumbed to the truth. Why hadn't he asked to speak with her? He'd seen enough movies to know that was proper procedure. Pay up in forty-eight hours and they'd be on a bus home unharmed. If not, no one was safe, including Frank. Were they unharmed even now?

The solution was well beyond Frank's capabilities, if not financially, certainly emotionally. He could manage to put that kind of money together but not in two days. Remortgaging the house and putting it together with what he had stashed would get him close, probably close enough to buy him some time, but in no way could that happen in forty-eight hours. To raise that kind of cash that fast would have to involve someone else. If his life was miserable now, it was nothing compared to what it would be. It would be a joke. No job, no family. Worst of all, he'd be broke. He ran fingers from both hands through his thick, graying, black hair. It had been years since he felt the warmth of tears fill his eyes and caress his cheeks but they were there now. He picked up the putter and began pacing again.

His thoughts turned to Allison and where she must be this minute. His love for her was borne of the familiarity of thirteen years of marriage. No longer was it driven by the smoldering passion he'd had when he was twenty-four. Still, he felt her pain and wished that he could ease it. His pain for Madison was deeper still. As he thought of her, he realized that this was his crowning achievement as a failure at being a father to her. By most standards he had been an adequate parent. He kept her warm and fed. Until now he had kept her safe. He never hit her. But he rarely talked to her, rarely nurtured her. As he filtered through the memories, he knew he had treated her as a necessary inconvenience of life. Much like shaving or changing the oil in your car.

The decision Frank came to was not because he didn't care but because he was simply challenged beyond his intellect or courage. It was not a decision he had come to lightly nor quickly, for it had been slowly coming into focus since the fateful game. It was still only three-thirty in the afternoon and the banks were still open. He could make his phone call, withdraw the cash and be at the airport in an hour. Cash for the ticket would be harder to trace and by the time anyone found out he'd flown to Mexico City, he would be well settled in some warm seaside hacienda many miles away.

He lifted the telephone once again and dialed the number.

"Birchwood Police Department," a gravely voice said on the other end of the line.

Frank sighed deeply, resignedly. "I want to report a kidnapping."

CHAPTER FOUR

4:05 p.m. Thursday

Martin Gerard pulled open the single drawer that hung beneath the heavy, unpolished oak table that served as his desk and removed the revolver. He pointed the weapon across the table at Carson who stood cowering in blanched silence.

"Can you give me one reason why I shouldn't just end your miserable fucking life right now? And being my wife's stupid, little brother doesn't count."

Carson made no response.

"Well?"

"Martin," Lonnie interjected, "not here, not now. We still need him to help with the search."

Gerard kept the gun pointed at his big henchman. "Really? You think you can count on this big ape to help? I don't think so. You'd think he would have learned his lesson but losing a finger wasn't enough. I'm gonna put him out of his misery."

"Aw c'mon, Martin," Lonnie pleaded, "I don't have time to clean up a body now. We've gotta find the women and that'll just slow me down. Please, let it wait. I'll keep an eye on him. Make sure he doesn't cause us anymore trouble."

Gerard shifted his gaze to Lonnie for a moment. He glanced back at Carson, still pointing the weapon at him, and said, "Bang." Then he put the gun back in the drawer.

"Did you put the crew on the streets?" he asked Lonnie.

"Brick's got it handled."

"It'd better be everybody. I don't want them hoppin' a bus or a cab, or sticking out their thumbs. And if they got to a phone…" He let the thought trail off but his hard gaze remained steady. Lonnie felt a bead of sweat escape from under his right arm and trickle down his side.

"Brick knows what to do. And there aren't any buses or cabs running in this weather."

"Does he? How about the street people?"

"That too."

"What kind of reward?"

When information was needed, the homeless that dotted the landscape in this part of city proved surprisingly resourceful. They seemed to have their hands on the pulse that ran through the many decrepit and depressed blocks that Gerard considered his territory. When knowledge was needed about the local goings on, they were more than willing to help Gerard. The rewards he offered from time to time were more than welcome but staying on his good side was the real goal. If you didn't, chances were that you couldn't lay low long enough to survive.

"The usual. A hundred bucks."

"Son of a bitch, Lonnie, does this seem like a usual situation to you?" Gerard couldn't hold his anger any longer. There was too much at stake this time. "We're not dealing with the usual scum here. We've taken a woman and her daughter hostage. They may be just fuckin' pawns to us, just bargaining chips, but you can bet your ass the cops'll care. They may not give a shit about the bettor but they fucking care when innocent people are involved. And they're not just innocent, they're fuckin' rich and they're from the suburbs." He pounded his fist on the table. "Think, dammit!"

Lonnie swallowed hard. "How much do you want the reward to be?"

"Make it two grand. That'll spread like Aids through those losers and nobody'll be able to make a move without us knowing about it."

Lonnie and Carson began moving toward the door. "Lonnie," Gerard called out, "you know you're the one in charge of this, don't you?" Lonnie nodded silently. "Failure to find these two is unacceptable."

After his two men left, Gerard just stared at the papers on his desk. The wagers and debts listed on those papers were insignificant compared to what Mayweather was into him for. The current situation made it impossible for him to focus. He pulled his six-foot four frame out of the chair and wandered over to one of the windows. He patted his wide girth just above his belt. He shook his head from side to side and silently cursed himself. He had taken the bet from Mayweather simply because the guy was a lawyer from Birchwood. He assumed from those facts only that the guy was well-lined and could cover. He had tried to tell himself at the time that he shouldn't take it. Christ, the guy had never bet more than fifty large before. And now he wanted to bet a half a mil? Idiot. He had taken a few bets that size before but they were from bettors with histories. Typically slowly increasing wagers and timely payoffs. A red flag always went up when someone jumped a bet big time.

And now he was beginning to second guess his decision to involve Mayweather's family. It was new territory for Gerard and it was risky. One bad decision followed by a second. Fucking idiot! He had put the screws to others before for welching and certainly didn't mind doing what was necessary to collect his money. He didn't even mind doing the dirty work himself, which, after all, he still enjoyed. But the others had always been the bettor. More than likely they wouldn't go to the cops. They weren't clean themselves or they had too much to lose if someone else knew about their habits. Mayweather had somehow been elusive and they didn't seem to have a choice. He had hoped he could depend on Lonnie but now he was second guessing himself about that, too.

He rubbed the goatee that covered his chin and tried to peer through the window. With the lights on in the office and no street lights to be found in this part of the city, he could see only snow flying close to the glass. He moved closer and leaned against the window with his hands cupped to the side of his face. Outside the snow was coming down hard and fast and the wind had picked up. After a moment he could make out the snowdrifts that were beginning to form against the buildings across the street. Charlotte was going to start worrying about him soon. She would be angry that he was going to be awhile. He picked up his cell phone off the table and punched in his wife's number. He hoped he could hold his tongue when she asked about her baby brother.

CHAPTER FIVE

5:13 p.m. Thursday

Allison studied the man while she waited for him to respond to her question. He had taken off his overcoat revealing an unbuttoned dark green wool sweater that she hadn't seen previously. Loose threads hung from the sleeves and there was a hole the size of a baseball underneath his left arm revealing a glimpse of the flannel shirt. A white undergarment of some sort peeked through the worn out knees of his jeans. If the bottom of his pant legs had ever had a hem there was no longer any evidence of it. In stark contrast to his clothing, his face wasn't haggard. His nose was strong, somewhat sharp. What she could see of his complexion looked healthy. She didn't know what to make of him.

"Those men you were with are trouble," the man said quietly. "*You're* in trouble."

"Why do you say that?" Allison queried. His matter-of-fact tone was frightening. She couldn't help thinking it signified truth in what he was saying.

He rubbed his hands together over one of the candles. "I know what they're like...what they're capable of."

"And what is that?"

The man glanced at the girl and then back at Allison. He shrugged his shoulders and then shook his head. It took a moment for Allison to realize that he didn't want to say anything in front of Madison.

"All right. So, if you're helping us why aren't you taking us somewhere so we can make a phone call?"

"We had to make sure that we got away from them first. By now, though, the word is out."

"What does that mean?"

"Those men you were with pretty much run this area of the city. By now he has his men out on the streets and, if Gerard's true to form, he's spread the word that there's a reward for information on your whereabouts. There's going to be a lot of people looking for you everywhere."

Allison found this hard to believe and she wrinkled her face, letting out a derisive puff of air. "What do you mean by people? What do you mean by reward?"

"I mean most everyone that lives in this area. You need to understand that Gerard has a lot of influence here. Almost everyone knows him. He makes sure of that." He held her eyes with his, trying to make certain she understood his meaning. "And reward means exactly that."

She stared back at him for a moment. "So you're not interested in the reward?"

A small smile creased his lips. "No, I'm not," he said simply.

Allison paused her questioning and tucked the blanket around her daughter. Madison's eyes were heavy and she laid her head across her mom's thighs.

"So if what you're saying is true, we can't simply walk out of here, find a phone at Sam's Bar and call the police and wait for them?"

"Yeah, let's do that," Madison interrupted, looking up at her mother.

"We will soon, honey," Allison responded to her daughter. She looked back up at the man. " If I'd known you were going to drag us all over the city, bring us here to this…whatever the hell this is, and then tell me I can't make a simple phone call, I would have gone to that woman we saw earlier. Surely, she would have let me use her phone."

"We were still too close to Gerard's place and they might very well have shown up before the police even got there. Besides, more than likely, the woman might not have let you use the phone if she even had one. Most of the people here live in fear. They're suspicious of anyone and anything. You don't understand what it's like here. The city equates police protection with a tax base. As you can imagine, there's not much here. Gerard and his men are allowed to run free and if they don't like you, you'd better leave because no one's going to protect you from them."

"What about those people living in those houses across the street? They must work and pay taxes. They live here. They must expect police protection from their community."

A small smile formed on the man's face again. "I haven't heard that word in a long time. Community is not a word that has any meaning here. Sure, some of them work, more don't and some of them work for Gerard. For the most part, though, they're ghosts, barely hanging on. Not more than a breath away from being...without things."

Allison thought about that for a moment. She could think of no response, nor any reason to keep the line of conversation going. It was all too hard to believe. She nodded toward Madison and said, "So, you dragged us here. I'm assuming you have some idea how to get us out of here."

"I know some places where it will be safe to make a phone call and wait."

Not that long ago, she was concerned that the cold and snow was going to be their death. But they hadn't died and, now, she wanted out of here. Staying here any longer with people she didn't know or trust made no sense. Getting Madison back home and safe as soon as possible was the only acceptable option. "Let's go then," Allison said as she started getting ready to rise.

"They're not that close to here. You need to warm up some and get your strength back."

"Look, I really appreciate what you've done but I don't want my daughter to have to stay here any longer than necessary. Come on, Madison, get your shoes and coat back on. We're leaving."

"If you just wait a couple of hours longer, the place we're going to should be more crowded and you won't stick out so much."

"I don't want to wait. I want to go now. Come on, Madison."

The girl was struggling with still-damp socks. "Mom, let's do what he says. I'm still cold."

"I know you are, babe, but we shouldn't be here. We have to leave." She looked back at the man. "If you won't show us where to go, we'll go alone."

He tried once again. "It's too early for there to be any sort of crowd at the place I'm taking you. The more people that are around the less chance we have of being noticed and the safer you'll be."

"I'll take my chances," she said sternly.

Convinced she was not to be persuaded, he rose silently and began pulling on his coat. He picked up the items that he had spread across the floor earlier and Allison noted the meticulousness with which he closed the wrapper on the crackers and folded the blankets. She wanted to scream at him to hurry but thought better of it. After all, this was his home. After he stored the items back where he had gotten them, he led them with the flashlight over to the box at the back of the room.

"Let me check first."

When the board was removed, snow blew into the room with a force that astounded all of them. Madison nuzzled up against her mother in reflex to the cold that swept in. The man had to brush a snowdrift aside to make room for their exit. He stepped back down off the box, snow still clinging to his face and hat, pulled his gloves off and held them out toward Madison.

"Here, I want you to wear these." When the girl hesitated, he looked over at her mother. "Please."

Allison nodded and Madison put them on. Though her little hands swam in them, her index and middle finger fell well short of the holes, they were instantly warmer and she was glad to have them. "Thank you. They feel good."

He gave her a warm smile and then guided her up onto the box and out of the hole. As Allison made her way through the opening she couldn't help but wonder at the man's kindness. Naïve experience couldn't help but wonder what he wanted. She also tried not to think about the history of those gloves and what pestilence might be hidden in their threads.

Waiting for the man as he struggled to replace the board and wheelbarrow, Allison and Madison grew cold quickly. Snow was coming down hard and the wind howled. Pulling up collars and turning backs to the wind did little to keep the frigid temperature from laying siege to their bodies. Allison knew they couldn't stay out long and that forced her decision. She took her daughter's hand and started leading her quickly toward Sam's Bar.

They were halfway across the vacant lot that separated the two buildings before the man realized what they were doing. He ran to try to catch up with them. He yelled to them, "Sam's isn't safe!" Even if his words had not been carried away so swiftly on the blustering winds, she would have ignored him.

Hunched over from years of being beaten down by life and those he couldn't seem to help crossing, Two Spoon looked into Brick's face with hungry eyes. His hands were clasped together in front of him, as if he were in prayer, a habit he had picked up years back when someone commented on the constant movement of his fingers. That habit had been caused by years of putting substances into his body that weren't on the Surgeon General's list of user friendly dietary supplements.

"Two big ones, man?"

Brick glanced at him with irritation and then looked around the bar, again. "Yeah, that's right," he said.

"A woman and a kid, right?"

"Yeah, that's what I said."

"I might have some information. Can I git somethin' up front?"

"Fuck no. You know how it works, little man. You got something that pans out, you get the money." Brick turned toward him. "And if you got something, you'd better be spilling it now."

"I might have somethin', but you need to show me some faith, brotha'. I'm not sayin' it has to be money. You know what I'm talkin' 'bout."

"What makes you think I've got something for you other than money?"

"Oh, c'mon, man. This is Two Spoon you talkin' to. I may be outta luck but I ain't outta sense."

Brick gazed at the smaller man, smiled slightly and shook his head. He disliked him but he did admire his audacity. And, somehow, he always seemed to have the low down. He leaned in toward Two Spoon and spoke evenly. "I'm going to give you a hit, little man, but you'd better come with something good or you're gonna wish you never came in here tonight."

Two Spoon's eyes were glistening at the thought of a hit. He adjusted his ratty Lakers ball cap further to the side and pulled down the dark blue material that served as a scarf around his neck in anticipation. "I wouldn't lie to ya, Brick, my man. Like I said, I might be outta luck but I still got sense."

Brick reached into his pocket and pulled out a small vial containing white powder. Without concern of being seen, he simply handed it to Two Spoon. The smaller man grabbed it greedily, turned the small handle on the bullet and started to put it to his nose. Brick stopped the movement.

"Don't you put that in your nose. I won't wanna use it again. Put it on your hand first."

Two Spoon did as he was told. Quite quickly he turned the handle a second time and began to put another line on his hand. Brick stopped the movement again.

"I said one."

"Oh, c'mon, man. I gotta do both holes. You gotta have symmetry."

Brick just looked at him for another moment and shook his head. He should have expected it. Otherwise, the guys nickname would be One Spoon. "You better have something good."

After the second hit, reluctantly, Two Spoon handed back the vial. He snuffed hard, grabbed his nose and wiggled it and snuffed hard again. "My man, Brick. You are that."

"So, let's hear it, little man."

"I saw a woman and a girl not more'n an hour ago who didn't look like they were from 'round here. Maybe four blocks from here. They were trailin' some guy I know."

"Four blocks in which direction?"

"That way, I guess," he said, pointing over Brick's right shoulder.

"Like near Washington where it crosses Paris?"

"I guess it could be. Yeah, that's right."

"I need you to be specific, Two Spoon. Which way were they headed? Now think."

"Okay, okay, yeah, yeah, it was near Washington and Paris. They were going down Paris, sort of, I guess. Toward downtown."

"What d'ya mean sort of? Were they going south?"

"Shit, I don't know what direction they were goin', man! They were headed downtown."

"Who was the guy they were with?"

"It was that Dogman guy."

"Dogman? Who the hell is that?"

"You don't know Dogman? I thought everybody knew 'im. You ask the street, they'll know 'im."

"Do you know where he hangs?"

"Nah. Nobody does. Ya just see 'im once in awhile."

Brick looked around the room, again, considering what he'd been told. After a moment he asked, "What else do you know?"

"Nothin' man. That's it."

Brick headed for the door.

"That's alotta information, don't ya think?"

Over his shoulder, Brick said, "Yeah, you did good, little man."

Two Spoon followed Brick toward the door that was already closing. "When you catch 'em, I get the reward, right?" Brick was already gone. Two Spoon turned back toward the room and started making his way to the wall opposite the bar trying to avoid being seen by the bartender, who would surely kick him out into the cold. "Yeah, that's right. I get the reward," he said to no one in particular.

The eighteen-year-old kid handed the phone back to Sam and nodded at him. It wasn't the typical nod where the chin goes downward in an abbreviated bow, usually meant as a thank you or a greeting or an okay, but the nod of a street-tough kid where the chin goes up, a more defiant form, but of acknowledgment only. In spite of the gallant efforts of the furnace in the basement of the bar and the roar of the overhead space heater located above the front window, the kid put his hood back over his head and sauntered toward the entrance.

At that same moment Allison and Madison were on the sidewalk in front of the bar. As much as she wanted to burst through the front door and let the warmth caress them, and as much as she wanted to burst in and scream for help, she hesitated, taking time to look through the only part of the window not fogged to opaque by the vastly different temperatures on either side. Her heart skipped a beat when she saw the pay phone mounted on the wall adjacent to the entrance. Just as she was about to move toward the door, the man grabbed her by the arm.

"I'm telling you, it's not safe." Steam came from his mouth like a locomotive and Allison noted that he'd had to run to catch up with them. "One of Gerard's men may be in there."

"There's a pay phone right inside the door," she said forcefully, "and I'm going to use it."

As she said this, she pointed toward it and both she and the man looked through the glass just as the hooded kid picked up the receiver. The kid glanced furtively around the bar and then viciously yanked on the receiver dislocating the cord from its source. Outside on the sidewalk Allison's head jerked at the sudden vandalism. The kid laid the receiver back in its cradle and glanced around the room again. The man tugged on Allison's arm.

"Come on. We've got to leave here."

She didn't move but kept staring through the window trying to comprehend what had just happened. She wasn't convinced that it had anything to do with her but she also couldn't convince herself that it was just coincidence either.

"We've got to leave," the man urged her, "He's going to come out that door any second."

Just before the kid opened the door he peered at the part of the window that was still translucent. Through the opening he saw nothing but blowing snow.

CHAPTER SIX

6:29 p.m. Thursday

News of the kidnapping of the Mayweather woman and her daughter hit the police departments of the greater Lordmont area quicker than a tantalizing grade school rumor spreads on the playground at lunch time. The police, of course, needed to know such information in order to protect citizens and keep tabs on the movement of the bad guys. Though not one officer would admit it, they also derived a certain amount of perverse pleasure from the stories. By six-thirty in the evening of the same day that Allison Mayweather found herself in the big city in the company of strangers, all officers on duty in every police department in the immediate vicinity of Birchwood, including Lordmont, had been briefed on the incident. Due to the fortuitous timing and location of an undercover officer working the downtown streets, they had more information than just the terse Frank Mayweather phone call. Thanks to forged friendships with those who knew the streets and were willing to impart their knowledge for little favor, they were fairly certain who had taken her, they had some sketchy information on the identification of the person she was now with and they knew about the reward. No one knew where she was.

At the police department in St. Lucille, two suburbs east and slightly north of Birchwood, Lieutenant John Draganchuk was on his way out the door. St. Lucille was a quiet upper-middle class town but it was the first decade of the new millennium and even the moderately affluent suburbs were strafed with enough crime to make police forces seem like skeleton crews. It had been a typically long day. He had gone without lunch again and if he didn't get home to Joyce soon and have dinner with her, there would be no reversing his rotten mood. The last thing he needed was to be stopped before he got out of the door.

"Drag, wait up."

The lieutenant's shoulders sagged as he stopped with his hand on the door. He turned around to face the uniformed officer and let out a long and obvious sigh. The uniform laughed at him. His gruffness was only a thin façade that concealed a very warm heart.

"Don't worry, you can go home. I just wanted to walk out with you."

"Good. Let's go then."

"You missed the briefing. Wanna hear about it?"

"If I said no then I suppose I'd have to make pleasant conversation with you all the way to my car, huh?"

The uniform laughed, again. "I sure hope you have to work on that sense of humor because if it comes with years on the job, I'm going into security work." When Draganchuk only muttered at the driving snow and pulled the collar of his overcoat around his neck, the uniform continued. "Anyway, a Birchwood woman and her daughter were taken hostage this afternoon by a Lordmont book."

"Gerard?" the lieutenant interrupted.

"The same. No one knows for certain but it's suspected the husband fell short on a bet and this is Gerard's way of making the stiff sit up and listen."

"That's not generally his m.o."

"It seems extreme, even for him. But get this. The word is that Gerard's men lost the hostages and they're somewhere in the city being led around by a guy from the streets."

"No shit?"

"That's the word. And he's put out a reward for information for two large."

Draganchuk shook his head as he opened the door to his vehicle.

"Every John Q's going to come out of the woodwork for that kind of money. LPD's going to have to get lucky to get to them first."

"Amen to that. Goodnight Lieutenant."

"Night. Say hello to Nancy and the kids."

"Will do. You do the same."

Just before Draganchuk got in his car, he asked, "They get an ID on the guy they're following?"

"Affirmative. He calls himself Dogman, or maybe it's The Dogman. Who knows?"

The lieutenant stopped his descent into his car quite suddenly. "Dogman?"

"That's affirmative, again. Why? You know the name?"

Draganchuk gazed at the uniform silently for a moment. "No," he lied and then got into his vehicle and drove home to Joyce.

"Goddammit!" Gerard spat into the phone, "You fuckin' lost him?" He listened to excuses for a few seconds. "No shit, Sherlock. I know it's fucking snowing." He paused for a moment, trying to think what to do next. This whole thing had become a disaster and Mother Nature was playing with him. "All right, you stay up there and stake out Mayweather's house until he shows but send Williams back here. We need everybody we can find on the streets." He nearly switched off the phone. "And don't let the cops find you sleeping in your car, you got it?"

He punched the buttons on the phone with such fury that he nearly knocked it from his hand. When Lonnie's cellular rang a second time he screamed at the phone impatiently.

"Yeah?"

The connection was poor and Gerard could barely hear through the scratching signal. "Lonnie, you there?"

"Yeah, I can hear you."

"What's going on? Anything new?"

"No. But everybody's out even though they're bitchin' about the cold."

"Good. How about the street people? You spread the word on the reward?"

"Yeah, but the weather's keeping a lot of them undercover. Even so, a lot of them are out looking for the end of the rainbow. I imagine there's going to be a few dead ones in a few hours or so, from exposure or whatever."

"Any police activity?"

"Not that I can see. Do we know that they know?"

"I don't know but I saw a couple of strange types loitering on the street outside the office. They could be watchin'. I haven't seen any cruisers. I wouldn't be surprised if one of 'em made a call by now."

"Even if they did, the weather's going to slow the cops down, too. There aren't going to be any vehicles on the streets for awhile. It's really coming down."

"Yeah, good." Gerard paused, feeling odd. His control over the situation seemed fleeting and the onslaught of snow and cold made him feel cut off from his men and trapped inside his barren office. He hadn't felt desperation since he was seventeen, already dropped out of school and looking to make his mark on the world. It was a suffocating feeling and he had a hard time speaking. "Lonnie, we gotta find those bitches. If the cops get to 'em before we do…well, fuck it all. I'd just as soon have 'em alive but the way I feel right now, if it's too much trouble, I'd just as soon the cops never find 'em. Know what I mean?"

Even with the bad connection, Lonnie could sense his boss's mood and he was almost embarrassed for the man. Weakness under any circumstances was only a harbinger of the end of your reign. "Yeah, I know what you mean. We'll get them, Martin. And, if need be, no one will ever find them."

Back in the cellar of the building across the vacant lot from Sam's Bar, the blankets were spread and the candles aglow, once again. The three of them sat silently trying hard not to stare at one another. Madison was not yet good at the art of staring inconspicuously or sitting quietly and she was making the man slightly ill at ease. As she lay with her head resting on her mother's crossed legs, she finally broke the silence.

"What's your name?"

He hesitated a moment before answering. Allison couldn't help but wonder if he'd forgotten. It didn't seem farfetched to her that a person living in such a state would lose track. Like struggling with your own phone number briefly because you never called it, could one forget one's own name after awhile if they never heard it? She didn't know if he had any friends. She guessed that he didn't need to fill out any forms with personal information.

"Robert."

"Do you live here?"

"Sometimes. I have other places I stay, too."

"Really? How many? Do you have a house?"

He smiled easily at her curiosity. "No, I don't have a house. But I've got five or six other places."

"Why do you have so many?"

Allison grew embarrassed at her daughter's inquisitiveness. She realized quickly it was only she that was embarrassed. Madison was simply acting like an eleven-year-old and Robert was answering nonchalantly without reservation. Even so, she thought, just because the man was helping didn't mean that he owed any personal information.

"Madison, I think that's enough questions. Why don't you close your eyes and try to take a nap."

"A nap? Mom, please, I'm eleven years old. I don't take naps anymore."

"That's quite all right," Robert interjected before Allison could respond to her daughter. "I have a lot of different places because I don't want anybody to be able to find me." With this last statement his voice grew to a whisper and his eyes widened, as if it were a matter of espionage.

"Really? Why don't you want anybody to find you?" Before he could answer, a look of concern came over her young face and she added, "Don't you want your family to find you?"

He thought a moment before answering. He now regretted being so flippant with the child. He was definitely out of practice. "I'm afraid I don't have any family, so there's no need to be found."

"What about your friends?"

"Well now, I let them find me, or I find them," he said with a wide grin.

Madison smiled back at him and then frowned in concentration. After a few seconds, she came up with another question. "Where do you shower and go to the bathroom?"

"Madison! That's not any of your business, young lady."

"I'm sorry," she said to Robert.

"That's all right," he said, "I use rest rooms here and there. I've gotten pretty good at sneaking in and out without being seen."

"How do you shower in a rest room?"

"Madison."

The man smiled at the girl. "I don't get to shower as often as I'd like but I can wash in all the right places pretty quickly. Have you ever heard of a pta bath?"

She had and she giggled.

Not that she wasn't interested, but Allison decided it was time to steer the conversation in a different direction.

"Madison, when you came running into the foyer this afternoon what were you yelling about?"

"Johnny Morton wrecked the snowman me and Jamie were building in her yard. We had it almost done when he came over and knocked it down. And when we tried to put it back together, he knocked it down again. So I hit him."

"Hit him? With a snowball?"

Madison lifted her head up from her mom's legs and looked at her. "No, I slugged him in the nose."

"With your fist?" Allison asked with exasperation.

She laid her head back down. "Yes."

"Madison, why on earth would you do such a thing? And where did you learn to do that?"

"Daddy taught me."

"I cannot believe you did something like that. We...at least I've tried to teach you that that is not how we settle arguments."

"It wasn't an argument. He was being mean and he wouldn't stop."

Allison let out a long sigh. "Did you hurt him?"

"I sure hope so."

Robert couldn't stop a brief laugh and Allison glared at him.

"Didn't you see if he was okay? Was he bleeding?"

Madison's eyes were growing heavy and she curled up a little tighter. "I don't know. We all ran home right after I hit him."

Allison played with her daughter's hair as she fell asleep. "We'll talk some more about this when we get home." The girl didn't respond.

With envy, the two adults watched the child slip into slumber. They were mesmerized by the innocence, a brief haven of escape from the stark reality that surrounded them.

After several uncomfortable minutes of silence, Robert said quietly, "I guess Johnny won't be bothering her anymore, huh?"

Allison looked down at Madison and shook her head slightly. She gazed back at Robert. "How much longer do we wait?"

He reached into the pocket of his overcoat lying next to him and pulled out a wristwatch that had no strap. "About an hour. It'll be eight o'clock then and there should be enough people for us to go unnoticed."

Although neither one said a word, both wondered if they could actually go unnoticed in this part of the city.

CHAPTER SEVEN

8:20 p.m. Thursday

Between five o'clock and eight o'clock that evening snow hit the ground in the city of Lordmont and its surrounding suburbs at the rate of three inches an hour. With four inches already on the ground, the total current accumulation now stood at thirteen inches. Meteorologists were prognosticating little easing of the icy siege until sometime in the wee hours of Friday morning. That much snow on its own creates havoc in a sprawling metropolis and slows any movement to a crawl, but the winds that gusted to forty-five miles per hour and drove the wind chill below zero were paralyzing. Fortunately, commerce, for the most part, was concluded for the day and the majority of rush hour traffic was safely home and tucked away in garages. Quite suddenly at a few minutes past eight, the winds died, taking the barrage of snow with it. Only a brief respite according to the local weather broadcasts. Now only a quiet smattering of small, crystalline flakes fell heavily to the ground. Temperatures remained at or near zero.

City fathers and the general populace were thankful that the storm didn't hit during business hours. Children all around the area were excited in anticipation of the coming snow day and the fun to be had outside. The snowplows hit the streets as soon as the storm ended. The salt trucks followed in their path. Moving that much snow so life could return to normal was challenging. In the middle of the city there were only so many places to push it out of the way. Hauling the snow away was a bit of a conundrum as it took vehicles to do so but vehicles found passage through the streets near impossible. The center of the city where commerce was heaviest would be cleared first but, still, would not see business as usual until mid to late morning. The part of the city where Allison Mayweather and her daughter were holed up was last on the priority list and, barring another onslaught of snow, the trucks would be lucky to begin their work in that area before noon the following day. Until then, the surrounding and seemingly endless city blocks of crumbling tenements, burnt-out buildings and other structures that somehow still stood well past their expiration dates would not see a moving vehicle unless it was equipped with treads normally seen on earth moving equipment.

During the last couple hours the board at the back of the building rattled with the wind and the temperature in the basement dropped. It remained somewhere around freezing, which was still significantly warmer than outside, but it was uncomfortable. At some point, Robert yielded the blanket on which he sat to the women. Allison protested for fear that he would freeze but he convinced her that he had gotten used to battling the cold for long periods of time. She eyed him curiously and from some deep recess of her mind came a scene from the old television program *Kung Fu*. Caine, the main character in the show, was forced to stay in a metal shed for a long period of time in unbearable heat. Through some ancient Asian wisdom he was able to focus his mind and body on ignoring the effects of the elements. Allison had strong faith in the power of the mind and she supposed it was possible for someone to withstand the cold, at least for awhile, anyway. And thus far the man seemed to have the demeanor of Caine. She had no way of knowing that during the first winter of Robert's time on the streets he had scraped together enough money to purchase top of the line thermal underwear from *Timberland*. She had expressed her gratefulness and snuggled beneath the blankets with her daughter. Despite the misgivings of her surroundings, she surrendered to the intensity of the day and actually drifted off to sleep. From time to time, Robert would rise and walk around the basement. Then he would sit again warming his hands close to the candles and gaze at his guests.

He didn't want to stare at them but he could not prevent it. It had been a long while since he had been in close proximity with people still in the game, and looking at their clean and unaffected faces brought feelings of nostalgia and a brief bout with remorse, feelings he hadn't had in many months. For as long as he dared, he bathed in the warm glow of remembering. The remorse he shrugged off easily.

Other than being an adult woman, Allison did not resemble Karen in any way. His guest's hair was to her shoulders and a light brown in color with blond streaks being picked up by the candlelight. Karen's hair was lopped off above the shoulders and was so black that in certain light it was a dark blue. Allison was neither tall nor short, whereas Karen was almost Amazonian in height, maybe a half inch taller than Robert's six foot one inch frame. But gazing upon her gentle and sleeping face, he couldn't help thinking of his former fiancee. It wasn't longing, however, because, no matter how he tried, he could never forget how or why their relationship had ended. Time had not yet done its job of suppressing the memory.

The stillness was different this time. He had come home before to find Karen not at home but those times her silent presence still somehow hung in the air, laying claim to the empty space. Nothing within his eyesight indicated that anything was different or out of place. Perhaps his senses were being jaded by another perfunctory job interview or, perhaps, it was last night's argument. What he felt now was certainly influenced by the distance that had wedged its way between them over the last few weeks. Other times, dare he say happier times, when he would make it home from work and she had not yet come from her own job, her aura was palpable within the walls of the two-bedroom apartment, as was the anticipation of her arrival. The atmosphere of the apartment now seemed cold and stark, almost unfriendly.

Robert Huntley had no real reason to believe what he was feeling but he couldn't help himself. He moved to the kitchen first. It seemed the safest. He stood in the archway with his back to the small living room, gazing over the linoleum surfaces. Everything looked as it had when he had left earlier in the day. He gingerly opened cupboard doors and drawers and peeked inside. As they had been for the past six months, every space, every crevice was jammed full with some form of kitchen implement. He had never known what half of the items were used for and had thought it was a waste of valuable space. He had felt this was also true for most of the other half since they were used only infrequently. At this moment, however, he was grateful for each and every one of them and decided right then and there that he would learn to use them. His spirit and hope began to climb out of their dark hole.

The apartment seemed markedly warmer as he made his way across the living room to the bathroom. He straddled the bowl and tried to stop himself from taking inventory in the small room. Just as in the kitchen, nothing was out of place. He almost made it out of the room without opening the medicine cabinet. Inside he saw the usual assortment of nonpharmaceuticals and hygiene products, both his and hers. Certainly, she couldn't leave without the necessities that resided within that cabinet.

Convinced now that he had let the negativity of the past few weeks wrongly color his current state of mind and that Karen would, in fact, be home soon in all her tall glory, he decided to return to the kitchen to open some wine. He hadn't glanced in the bedroom the first time he passed by on his way to the bathroom. On his way back to the kitchen he did. Standing in the middle of the living room, he was frozen, his feet seemingly cemented to the floor. He wanted to ignore what had caught his eye. He tried to assure himself it was just a piece of paper inadvertently left on the bed. But he knew it wasn't the piece of paper that made his heart grow heavy in his chest. It was the shiny object that lay on top of the piece of paper that had caught his eye.

When the winds outside quieted, Robert decided it was time to go. He placed his hand tentatively on Allison's shoulder and shook her gently.

"It's time to go."

Her eyelids fluttered delicately, fighting to stay open. When reality forced its way through the haze of sleep, her eyes popped open and she was instantly alert.

"Madison, time to wake up. What time is it?"

"Eight-twenty," Robert responded.

Madison sat up and put her hands to her eyes trying to rub the sleep from them. "What're we doing?"

"We're going to call someone to come and get us so we can go home."

"Can we go home soon? I'm cold."

"I know you are, honey," Allison said, avoiding a direct answer to her daughter's question, "Come on now. Get your shoes and socks on."

When the board was removed this time no wind blew in but the colder temperature outside made its presence felt quickly. A moment ago when Allison was coming from under the blanket and putting on her overcoat, she was miserably cold and wondered how much longer she could stand it. When the outside air fell heavily into the basement, she panicked briefly and considered crawling back under the blankets. She knew she and Madison could not subject themselves to the weather for long dressed as they were.

"How far is this place?"

"It's going to take about twenty minutes to get there."

"You've got to be sure. We're not dressed for this and I don't want her out in this weather any longer than she has to be."

"I'm certain. And it will be less if we're not forced to take detours."

As if where she was currently standing and what she and Madison were about to undertake wasn't enough to remind her of their predicament, Robert's last statement hammered it home. She began to hit the panic button again and froze for a moment. She shook it off, adjusted Madison's clothing to make sure it was covering as much of her as possible and said, "Let's go, then."

When the three of them ducked through the loose boards in the eight-foot wooden fence at the back of the vacant lot adjacent to Sam's Bar, it was as if they had entered a void. Behind them now, the fence blocked the meager light given off by the bar's faltering neon sign and, despite the whiteness of the snow, there was no light of any kind. Normally, there was little activity in this part of the city, less at night, and now the snow not only lessened what activity there might have been, it also muted all sound. Hand in hand, Robert led them through the blackness waiting for their eyes to adjust. The only sound was their footfalls.

The Shamrock Tavern was in its eighty-ninth year of business, having been opened, as the name intimates, by an Irish immigrant during the first World War. The fact that The Shamrock had outlasted almost every place of business in the near vicinity was not so much a testament to the entrepreneurial shrewdness of the line of Callahans that had run the place over the years as it was a tribute to the alcohol industry and its nearness to the heart of the local citizenry. The ever-decreasing number of residents nearby may not have the means to keep the neighborhood restaurant or hardware store in business, but when it came to the local bar, money for drinks was no problem.

On this particular night, The Shamrock was more crowded than usual. A normal crowd was maybe twenty-five to thirty people but tonight the number approached fifty. Customers who frequented the bar were locals within walking distance, so conditions as they were, driving was not an issue anyway. The storm was a fresh topic for discussion, giving the patrons a reason, legitimate or not, to convene, much like the World Series or a newly elected President.

Robert was pleased when they walked into the bar. He wasn't sure what to expect because of the storm, but the crowd was more than he had hoped. Dismay came rapidly, however, when, despite the jovial clamoring, for it was a small bar and the door was within almost everyone's eyesight, many of the heads, particularly those seated close, turned when the three entered. He tried to convince himself that they didn't stare any longer than they normally would at new arrivals but failed. It was unsettling and he tried his best to ignore it for the benefit of the women. He nonchalantly herded them to an open table near to the door they had just come through. He had to raise his voice to be heard above the din when he told Allison that he would be right back. She grabbed his arm before he left and looked at him with eyes that tried to be steely, but the fear in them couldn't be concealed. She had gotten used to his company and wasn't ready to be without it in this foreign place. He patted her hand and told her again that he would be right back.

Robert mentally kicked himself for his foolishness. A street person, a woman from suburbia and a kid, all very obviously dressed for their parts. How could he have possibly thought they could sneak in unnoticed? In fact, he surmised, he might very well be the one that's drawing the attention. While the women might be strangers, at least they were dressed somewhat appropriately. It was he who was drawing the many disgusted looks.

In his haste to act quickly, Robert turned toward the bar and nearly ran into someone carrying an empty tray. Robert apologized to the young man, who smiled back and told them that he'd be with them in just a moment and then disappeared through a door that had the word *office* stenciled on it. Robert headed for the bar telling himself that running into people was not in the least bit maintaining a low profile.

Billy Callahan saw Robert approaching and a broad smile appeared on his beefy reddened face. As a rule, he hated street people and would kick them out of his place as soon as they came in, but Robert was different. He never came in looking for odd jobs or something free, and he never came in just to get out of the weather. Not that he saw him much, maybe every three or four months, but when he did come in he always had money for a drink. One drink. That's all he would have and no matter how Billy tried to push another his way, Robert never took it. From the day they met, Billy learned Robert was different from the other homeless. Many months ago on a scorching summer day, Billy was attempting to lug a small freezer through the front door of The Shamrock by himself when Robert happened by and took it upon himself to pick up the other end. His ragged clothes gave Robert away and, not wanting to be beholden to him, Billy told him he had it and didn't need the help. Robert smiled at him and told him he already had the thing picked up and could they get going because it was getting heavy. When Billy thanked him that day he was expecting to have to part with some food and drink but Robert only told him that he was welcome and went on his way. To this day, Billy has never gotten Robert to accept anything for free.

"Robert! Good to see ya. What brings you by here this snowy night?" Billy held out a large hand that was even beefier than his face.

Robert took his hand and leaned on the bar to get closer to him. He glanced at the customers sitting close to where he stood making certain they were occupied. "Billy, I need to use your phone. Is that possible?"

"Sure it is. Is there somethin' wrong?"

Robert gazed at him a moment measuring his response. "No. I just need it this one time. I hope you don't mind."

Billy came out from behind the bar, walked up to him and discernibly glanced toward the women and then back. "I heard some things. You're not gettin' yourself into somethin' you might not be able to get out of, are you Robert?"

He'd seen how far Gerard's influence could go many a time since he'd been in this part of Lordmont but it still never ceased to amaze him how quickly word could spread when Gerard wanted it to. He worried now that this may not be the safe haven he had hoped for. "It's a little late for that now," Robert finally answered.

Billy looked at Robert for a long moment, the worry in his eyes evident. "You watch your back, my friend." He then put his hand on Robert's shoulder. "Come on, let's go to the office."

As they walked back past the table where Allison and Madison sat, Billy smiled amiably at them and nodded. Robert gazed curiously at a man who was trying to engage Allison in conversation. He smiled to himself imagining she had never heard the kind of pick up lines that were used on this side of the tracks.

The door to the office swung inward and Robert followed his large friend through the door. The man on the phone, the same man carrying the tray that Robert had almost run into, didn't see the two enter.

"I'm tellin' ya', Brick, they're here right now."

Billy and Robert wordlessly backed out of the room together, shutting the door as they went. Billy turned to Robert and said as quietly as he could, "You'd better get goin'."

Robert walked directly to the table. "Come on, we've got to go now." His eyes were locked on Allison's trying to make her understand the urgency.

She saw it and immediately rose. "Come on, honey, we're leaving."

Madison liked the warmth of the bar but she sensed the aura of seriousness given off by the adults and began to get up, too. Besides, she was too weak to protest.

The man who had been at the table trying to drag Allison into conversation was suddenly noticeable and standing menacingly between the party of three and the door. "Why don't y'all just have a seat for awhile."

Wasting any time at all was not an option. He had no idea how close Gerard's men might be to the bar. The man standing in front of the door wasn't any bigger than Robert. He was definitely shorter. Acting on pure instinct, Robert put a left jab into the man's nose so quick that he even surprised himself, not to mention the other man. He then grabbed him by the front of his green army field jacket and flung him toward the center of the room, his momentum toppling him over a metal-legged chair and to the ground. The patron, whose chair had been jostled, stood up and started yelling at the man on the ground.

Robert turned back to Allison. "We've got to go quick," and then pushed them toward the entrance. Just before he exited the bar he glanced back at Billy who was still standing in front of the office door. The door was open now and tray man was trying unsuccessfully to get by the big man. Their eyes met and Billy nodded almost imperceptibly at Robert.

CHAPTER EIGHT

9:18 p.m. Thursday

Light emitting from the flashlight splashed off the walls and ceiling, revealing nothing except the closeness of the cement block on either side and above. Colors were only shades of black and white. It was impossible to discern the color of the brick or the occasional caged fixture that once held incandescent light bulbs. The smoky air was palpable in its thickness. Godforsaken came to mind as Allison stumbled along between her two companions. From time to time, she would trip by running up the back of Robert's feet, trying to stay as close to him as she could in this unearthly place. Madison's fingernails were digging into the palm of her left hand. She knew her little girl was scared to death. And why shouldn't she be in this place? You couldn't see, you could barely breathe, and judging by the width of whatever space it was they were walking in, passing by someone coming in the other direction would be an intimate adventure. She wanted to vent a claustrophobic scream but she sensed the thickness of the air would only mute the sound. If and when she got out of this mess, she promised herself that she would make certain that Madison would forever be safe and warm.

The only redeeming factor of the current state was that they seemed to have escaped the bitter cold. The trek from The Shamrock had taken almost thirty minutes and had taken place in temperatures that were at or below zero in drifted, knee-length deep snow and thirty-mile-per hour gusts of wind. But she took little solace from the mildness for she worried the atmosphere they were in now might be less healthy. She feared the warmth they felt came from a combination of steam and smoke. She didn't know the source of the steam but she knew it could carry with it things not seen by the human eye. The puddles they splashed through periodically made her think of vermin, which only increased her fears regarding the steam. The smoke came from the three barrels of burning trash they had passed just before they entered the corridor. The fifteen or twenty people huddled around the barrels was her first stark view of the world she had entered. Until now, she had only had contact with a man who, except for his manner of dress, could pass as normal. The people she had just seen, which, much to her dismay, included several children, were certainly dressed in garb much more ragged than what Robert wore but that was not what shocked her. It was their faces. Allison saw the three or four that turned toward them as they passed the barrels and caught glimpses of others. Their faces showed nothing at all. Even in the minimal light given off by the fires she could see the lifeless eyes, the passionless mouths. Their faces were virtually indistinguishable from one another. When she looked at these people, and it was only momentarily as they passed, forgotten was the thought that permeated her being. These people were forgotten. Forgotten by families, forgotten by the social system, forgotten by society. Left in its wake.

They turned a corner to the right and made their way down another corridor. Thirty feet later Robert stopped abruptly and Allison once again ran into him. Pointing his flashlight to his right into a recess in the wall, two steps were revealed that led upward to a metal door. A sign was riveted to the door but whatever word or words that once appeared on it were no longer legible. They walked up the steps and through the door. They were no longer in a narrow hallway and the air cleared of smoke. Allison chased the beam of light around the room as Robert moved about and caught views of more cement block. The room appeared to be empty. The area was large, maybe fifty feet from the door where they had entered to the opposite wall. The ceiling looked to be twelve feet high. About two-thirds of the way across, the room was divided by floor-to-ceiling chain link fencing. Off to one side, there was a door in the fencing made of the same material and another smaller door in the middle three feet from the floor. Robert opened the door in the fencing, walked a few feet and bent down out of sight behind a long wooden counter that ran the width of the room behind the chain link. When he stood back up he told the women to come through the door to his side of the barrier. Just as he had at their last place of refuge, he spread a sparse picnic of candles and wool blankets on the cement floor.

Except for The Shamrock, the temperature here was warmer than what she had experienced since she had escaped the heat of the Lincoln. But it did little to soothe her. This place was dank. At least when it was cold, disease seemed less likely. She had hoped not to see blankets and candles on a cold and hard cement floor again. She was having trouble comprehending why it was so difficult to make a lousy, goddamn phone call to have the police come and rescue her and her daughter. She questioned the man's ability to protect them, following him through this hell hole of a city. She was questioning, once again, her decision to leave her original captors. She and Madison seemed hostages even now. Just a different captor. They were still cold, they were still wet, they were tired, they were in the dark and for all she knew they were lost. In danger or not, they would probably have been more comfortable with the others. And her daughter's comfort was what mattered most. She was now pissed off.

"What the hell was that all about at the bar? You said there wouldn't be any problem making a phone call." Allison threw her arms out in frustration and her voice was raised. "And what the hell is this place? A goddamn cave? It's dark and it's damp. I don't want to sit on cement anymore. I want to put some dry clothes on my daughter. We're hungry. I'm…"

She stopped abruptly. Robert had been gazing at Madison and when Allison finally looked down at her, she realized the girl was crying.

"Oh, honey," she breathed, going to one knee and hugging the girl to her, "we're going to be all right. We'll get back home soon. We'll put on some warm, dry clothes. You'll see."

"I wanna go home now," Madison managed through her tears. "I don't like it here."

Allison brushed the auburn hair from the girl's face. "I know. We will soon. Just a little while longer." She could feel Madison shaking and she held her tighter. "You know what you could do for me?"

"What?"

"Take off your shoes and socks, and your coat, too, and get between these blankets. Get nice and snuggly and you'll warm up in no time. Okay?"

"'Kay."

As she helped Madison get as comfortable as one could under the circumstances, she spoke to Robert. She did her best to maintain her tone while she glared at him. "So what now? Have you got a plan?"

Robert ignored the sarcasm in her voice. "I know another place we can try. It should be safer."

"Safer?" Allison struggled to hold the anger from her voice. She didn't want to upset Madison anymore than was necessary. "I thought the place you just took us was supposed to be safe."

"I thought it would be. The guy who owns the place is a friend of mine."

"Some friend," she said, the sarcasm returning to her voice.

He didn't respond immediately. Allison thought he looked hurt by the comment but she was less concerned about insulting him than she was earlier. She needed to get out of here.

"He wasn't the one that called Gerard," Robert said evenly, looking her in the eyes. "It was one of his employees. And, in fact, he helped us get out of there."

It was the first time that she had heard any kind of tone out of him that wasn't deferential. She thought back to The Shamrock and the violent act he had committed earlier against the man that blocked their exit. She realized she had no idea who Robert really was or what acts he was capable of committing. She softened her tone.

"All right. So what makes you think this next place is going to be any better? How does everybody know about this?"

"Like I said. Gerard…"

"I know. I know. He's f… he's everywhere. How about those people we passed on our way in here? Aren't they going to call Gerard and tell him where we are?"

"No."

"Why not?"

"They're …ah…they just don't leave here much. I'm fairly certain that they haven't even heard about it."

"But I thought Gerard's influence spread all over the area," Allison interrupted, holding up two fingers on each hand to represent quotation marks. Her frustration at the continuing less than satisfactory answers to her questions made it impossible to stop the sarcasm and anger from returning to her tone of voice.

Robert gazed at her thoughtfully for a moment, supposing she had a right to be angry. He hadn't exactly delivered her out of harm's way and dragging her here was not something on which he had planned. Actually, if asked, he would have said he had no plan past The Shamrock. He was now making it up as he went. "We're farther away and his influence is weaker out here. Those people you saw, by the barrels, they don't go on the streets that often. In fact, many of them don't go out at all. Those that do venture out don't go very far. Even if they had heard about it, which is doubtful, they just wouldn't care."

"I don't understand. Why wouldn't they care about a reward? They don't have any money, right?"

"No, they don't. Some might care but for most of them, they've been here so long that it's all they know. The reward means nothing to them."

"I still don't understand."

"Many of those people you just saw have been out of society so long they no longer have the desire to be in it. Some have never even been in it because they're children or they've been here since they were children. This is their society and they don't want anything to do with the outside world. They wouldn't know how to interact with it. It frightens them."

"How do they survive?" His words had chased away her anger. She had a hard time believing what she was hearing. "How do they eat? Where do they sleep?" The questions that peppered her mind were endless.

"Like I said, a few of them venture out and bring back whatever food they can find, and other supplies. Other times, particularly around certain holidays, rescue missions bring food in or, at least, close by. They sleep wherever they can. What you don't understand is that this is all they know or what they've gotten used to. For many of them...for most of them, their life is right here, particularly the children or those who've been here since they were born. I hate to even say it because it sounds so sad, but they're like a colony of ants. You see a few of them from time to time on the surface, but the vast majority is always underground out of sight."

Allison's mouth was agape. "You mean to tell me that babies are born down here and this is where they grow up?"

"I'm not saying it doesn't happen. But more often families with young children end up here. They can't find a way out, so they stay. And a lot of the time their kids end up staying with them. In turn, the kids don't get educated and they don't get acclimated into society. These people have truly fallen through the cracks. And they've fallen so far that getting them back is nearly impossible."

Allison battled internally. She tried to focus on her own problems. Knew that's what she should do. Madison had no one else to depend on, after all. What Robert had just told her weighed on her heavily. She had witnessed the faces of the people they spoke of. The visualization was much clearer. It was now reality. It wasn't just words read in a newspaper or heard on a television, anymore. It rendered her speechless for several moments.

After awhile Allison spoke, although it was closer to a whisper in deference to Madison's heavy eyelids. "What makes you believe the next place will be safer?"

"It's further from Gerard's territory. I know the owner pretty well."

"How far is it from here?" she asked reluctantly.

"In these conditions, it could be thirty, thirty-five minutes."

Allison shook her head, a look of anguish on her face. "I can't keep letting Madison run around in this weather." She reached out and touched her daughter's long socks that were spread by one of the candles. "Her socks are soaking wet. Her shoes are wet clear through. She doesn't have clothes that are warm enough. I can't keep doing this."

"I know. I'm sorry for that. Maybe you two should stay here and I'll go alone. I..."

"You are not leaving us alone in this place," she whispered, but it sounded more like a hiss. "I have no idea where we are. Hell, I'm not sure I could even get us out of this building."

"I can travel faster alone. The three of us stand out too much. At least you'll be warm enough here. I won't have any trouble getting there and back."

"Yeah, well, what if you do? What am I supposed to do then? No."

Robert gazed at her for several seconds. He pulled his time piece out of his coat and finally acquiesced. "All right. It's almost nine forty-five now. Dry out as much as you can for a half-hour or so. We need to get there before eleven. He normally keeps the place open later than that but with this weather he might decide to close early."

They both tried to get comfortable once again. They both removed their boots. Hers, which were beige when the day began, were now a dull gray from the wetness. His were mismatched. The one on his left foot was a hiking boot in relatively good shape. The right was a simple suede overshoe with a zipper instead of laces. It featured the flapping-sole look. After her coat was removed, Allison took as much of the blanket as she dared and still not disturb Madison, who was quietly drifting.

She looked around the room, her eyes having adjusted to the semi-darkness. There was another metal door close to them in the wall opposite the door they had entered. The remainder of the room and the wooden counter were completely empty.

"Won't your friend be in trouble with Gerard for helping us?"

"Billy? No," Robert said, laughing softly, "He's from a big family. There's a lot of them and they all seem to be as big as he is. In fact, I think he might be the smallest. Their family has been around here forever and they're strong-willed and tight-knit. Gerard won't mess with him because then he'd have to deal with the whole family."

She nodded her head thoughtfully gazing around the room some more. "What is this place?"

"It's the old Department of Public Works building. It hasn't been used for over forty years, although, the sewer lines…"

Robert stopped in mid-sentence when they suddenly heard a muffled voice on the other side of the door closest to them. Then they heard something bang hard against it.

As he went south on the Rutgers freeway, the lieutenant slowed the '01 Chrysler Concorde to a crawl to keep the car from running into the guard rails on the right or the low-lying median on the left. He was still enchanted with the vehicle's aging look but right now he cursed it for riding so low to the ground. The car struggled to drag itself through the powder. Hitting the accelerator only caused the front wheels to chew through the snow following the path of least resistance, which, it seemed, was random. It had started snowing heavily again and the traveling was going to be treacherous and slow. No use getting himself cracked up before he even got downtown. He buckled his seat belt and settled back.

Joyce hadn't said a word. He had known she wouldn't try to stop him, though, they both knew he wasn't suppose to be getting involved. First of all, it was *so* not his jurisdiction and second of all, it was personal. It could cost him his badge, might put him back in uniform, but he couldn't help himself. Joyce knew that too and that's why she hadn't protested. She listened to him quietly, looked at him hard with eyes filled with understanding and concern, kissed him meaningfully on the lips and then made him go upstairs and put on his thermal underwear while she filled an oversized thermos with hot black coffee.

Until today, it had been several months since he had thought about Robert Huntley. He had been gone now for how long, Draganchuk tried to think, maybe two years? He supposed over that length of time that you just start to forget things but he also supposed that he tried not to think about Robert because of the strangeness of his disappearance.

He had been such a good friend. There was no way to figure it out, no way to make sense of it, and that, at least for Draganchuk, actually made it painful to think about.

They had been friends for years, playing softball in the spring and summer, frequent lunches throughout the year, Robert helping him with taxes in the winter. Draganchuk had thought they had been close, at least as close as men got, but Robert had gone off without a word and that hurt, at first. But as time went on he found out that none of the other friends within their circle had gotten a chance to talk with him during that last winter before he was gone, either. The lieutenant eventually grew to understand why. It wasn't exactly the type of career move that you would discuss with friends beforehand and they all realized that they couldn't imagine what was going on in Robert's mind to cause such a withdrawal. It was mystifying to say the least. Before the trouble with Robert's business began, he and Karen had seemed happy. They looked like any of the other couples in their group. When the job interviews proved fruitless and the foreclosures started, he changed. He became sullen and reserved, which was quite unlike him. Karen left him not long after that and moved back home, wherever that was. Her disappearance was only slightly less strange.

Not long after it had happened Draganchuk had reached out to other officers in other departments for any word on Robert Huntley. For months there was nothing and eventually Draganchuk had stopped dwelling on it. A year and a half ago or so an officer out of Lordmont, who was also a friend of the lieutenant's, had overheard a bar owner refer to a homeless man as Robert. Several questions later it became evident that his friend had been located. Draganchuk briefly considered hunting him down but decided against it. He concluded that Robert just didn't want to be found.

The snow was deepening but not yet packed and the wheels on the right side of the Concorde bit through the powder and contacted the rumble strips along the edge of the pavement, jogging the lieutenant from his mental meanderings. He checked the slowly oncoming exit sign and figured he still had a good ten miles to go, which was going to take at least a half hour at the current rate of speed. He glanced at his watch and saw nine forty-five PM. The green sign announcing

Indianapolis Boulevard passed idly overhead and brought a smile to Draganchuk's face. He remembered a police softball tournament in which he had to talk Robert into impersonating an officer so he could participate. In a motel room outside of Indianapolis Robert and another civilian type were solemnly sworn in as deputies with a softball bat in their right hand and a brown long-neck in their left.

He tried to pay attention to the task at hand and fight off the memories that began to flood his mind. Involuntarily, Draganchuk felt the weapon under his heavy, dark green parka on the left side of his chest. He had his own with him tonight, not his service revolver. If anything went down, paperwork would be unnecessary. Other than Joyce, no one knew where he was going. Tonight was strictly an off-the-record assignment. He patted the right pocket of the parka feeling for the extra ammunition. He glanced at his image in the rear view mirror. The red and white stocking cap with Detroit Red Wings emblazoned in black on either side covered most of his brown and gray hair. He didn't want to look like a cop tonight, but that was the easy part. The hard part would be not acting like one.

CHAPTER NINE

10:01 p.m. Thursday

Madison leaned into her mother and Allison instinctively draped an arm around her shoulder hugging her close while Robert warily edged toward the door. Quite suddenly, fervent scratching against the metal, echoing loudly off the surrounding bare surfaces, could be heard on the other side. The noise, so loud and seemingly so out of place, caused Allison to tighten her embrace on Madison who was now attempting to bury herself inside her mother's clothing. Before Allison could stop him, Robert was already opening the door, the only barrier that protected them from whatever was making the foreign sound.

As soon as there was a crack in the door, the muzzle of a light colored dog impatiently forced its way through and bounded into the room. The obvious delight in the dog's face and manner and the way it nuzzled Robert caused little alarm in the women when it excitedly approached them, sniffing them from head to toe. The dog stood waist high to a typical adult human. Next to Madison, the dog could lick the girl's chin while keeping both paws planted on the floor. Or, to Allison's way of thinking, nip it. Madison giggled and started to reach out her hand but Allison pulled it back.

"It's all right," Robert said reassuringly, "She's the most harmless dog I've ever known."

While the dog forced its affections on the females, distracting them, a man entered the room a few moments later and exchanged greetings with Robert. Before long both women noticed the man and their concern began anew. He showed them a generous smile and walked toward them doffing his black stocking cap.

"May I introduce myself to you ladies? I assure you that I am as harmless as this silly canine." His voice was deep and raspy. It was ravaged from years of marginal health yet had a soothing calmness to it. He bowed slightly at the waist as he spoke. "My friends, which include your host, refer to me as Einstein. And may I say, despite these dreadful circumstances, it is a pleasure to make your acquaintance."

In spite of herself and, as he had said, their situation, Allison found it difficult to maintain her hard countenance. His eloquence indicated he was educated, though, she found it hard to imagine, given his dress and his presence here. At the moment, the strange man's pleasantness and politeness were impossible to resist. She could not help but smile back at him and take his hand. "My name is Allison and this is my daughter, Madison."

Einstein looked down at them for a moment. "I am truly sorry for your predicament. It is a sad statement which, unfortunately, speaks with accuracy to the state of today's society." His voice was warm but he spoke with sadness. "It is also unfortunate that your plight is rather well publicized in this dubious community of ours. However, you can rest assured that Dogman here will lead you to safety. No one knows this vicinage better than he."

Madison understood very little of what this new man had said but she liked him, anyway. The dog was also a welcome diversion and she was now focusing her attention on it. Allison looked at Robert questioningly. She now wondered how this new stranger and the dog were going to affect their attempted flight to safety. She also wondered why he had referred to Robert as "Dogman." Einstein continued to look down at the women. His fascination with them was strong, much like Robert's had been earlier. He shook his head, clearing his thoughts and turned to Robert.

"Dogman, sir, I have a gift for you."

He removed the worn, green canvas backpack that had been slung over his left shoulder and reached his hand inside. He pulled from the backpack a boot made of black leather that resembled those worn by the military.

"Although it is a size too large, somewhat scuffed and certainly in need of a spit shine, you will find that it is very well intact and will make a splendid replacement for that raggedy overshoe that you now wear."

Robert took the boot from him and examined it for a moment. "This is a fine boot, E, thanks."

"Wear it in health," Einstein replied.

The women watched with fascination as Robert went through the process of changing his boot. Not that a man taking off one boot and putting on another was normally fascinating, but nothing seemed to be normal anymore. The boot Robert had been wearing on his right foot was made of suede and was supposed to be secured over the foot by a zipper that ran up the front. The zipper was no longer serviceable and Robert had secured the boot to his foot with a shoelace tied around the outside. To prevent the shoelace from riding up and, thus, letting the boot fall open, he had found it necessary to also wrap the shoelace around the bottom of the boot, much like one might wrap a Christmas present so that the ribbon cannot slide to one side. When he finally managed to untie the knot, made less manageable by the snow that had caked to it, he removed the boot to reveal a plastic bag in its place. He pulled the bag off his foot and stuffed it inside the discarded boot and began to put on the new one. He stopped abruptly, took the new boot off, retrieved the plastic bag and put it over his foot again before donning the new boot. When he finished tying the new shoelace he looked up to see the other three staring at him. Only the dog seemed not to be paying attention to him. She was finding Allison's beige and gray boots much more interesting.

Madison broke the silence. "What's the plastic bag for?"

Einstein laughed earnestly. "The curiosity of children. It is dismissed so easily as impertinent. Pray tell, Dogman, what is the importance of the plastic bag?"

"The plastic bag doesn't let water get through and it traps a little heat. I needed it with the old boot because it obviously had a big leak." He picked up the suede overshoe and flapped the loose sole at her and smiled. Madison giggled. "I'm going to use it with the new boot because the new boot is not as well insulated as the old one and I need all the help I can get to keep my feet warm."

After the brief excitement of the new arrivals and the changing of the boot subsided, silence settled over the group. The adults watched Madison play with the dog for a little while, no one sure of where to go next. Finally, the girl realized how quiet it was and, being a child and generally not being able to stand the quiet for periods longer than several seconds, she, once again, broke the hush.

"What's the dog's name?" she asked Einstein.

"Her name is Yellow."

The animal, upon hearing her name, turned her attention from the girl and walked her sixty-five pounds toward Einstein. Yellow wagged her tail as she went, a movement the dog seemed unable to accomplish without moving its entire back end from side to side. The women couldn't help but smile at the comical walk.

"That's a funny name. Why do you call her that?" Madison inquired.

"Actually, this fine animal belongs to Dogman," Einstein replied, while at the same time trying to prevent the dog from nuzzling his crotch. "He should be the one to respond to your query."

"I'm not sure who belongs to whom," Robert said, watching the dog saunter back to Madison, "I think it's more a matter of her allowing me to provide for her. Anyway, I call her Yellow because she's mostly that color."

Allison spoke up at that point. "And he refers to you as Dogman because...?"

"Because I'm generally accompanied by the dog."

"And is your real name Einstein?" Allison asked, turning to look at the man.

The man gazed idly at Allison, stroking the graying, black beard of tight curls that covered his face. His deep brown eyes twinkled.

"Uh oh," Robert muttered.

"Unlike what scholars would have you believe, reality is quite fleeting, actually. Particularly in this part of the world. There are those that believe reality is simply perception. The concept of Hell is a perfect example. As you know, there are many who believe that Hell exists. You may be one. But certainly, no one knows whether it truly exists or not because there is no proof of its existence. Does that matter? No. For those who have been convinced that they will spend an eternity in Hell for their sins here on earth, it is a reality despite the fact that they cannot see it, smell it, hear it or feel it. There are others who do not believe in its existence. These people feel that it is a concept of fear, a manifestation created by those who wish others to live by a certain code of conduct. Does that make these people wrong because they believe something different? How can they be wrong if the existence of Hell cannot be proven? There are others, still, who believe that Hell exists here on earth. Their belief is that in a past life they perpetrated unforgivable sins upon mankind and, as punishment for such acts, this life is to be spent enduring misery. Where is the error of their judgment when they live in Hell everyday? So you see, those are three different beliefs in the same concept and each one is just as real as the other."

"Hey, E," Robert interrupted when his friend finally stopped to take a breath, "why don't you just answer the woman's question?"

"My apologies, ladies. Rhetoric is one of my weaknesses. In answer to your query, yes, Einstein is as real a name as any other name I might have gone by in…"

Robert interrupted him again. "He's called Einstein because, as you might have guessed by now, he's an intelligent sort." He glanced over at his friend with a smirk on his face. "Although, that may only be perception and not reality."

"The fact that my friends refer to me as Einstein may be more indicative of the level of their knowledge rather than my own."

Allison could see by the exchange between the two men that they seemed to have a typical friendship. She found it curious that she was surprised, after all, it was absolutely normal. She was oddly gladdened that such a friendship could exist in such abnormal circumstances. She considered the names that the men used to refer to each other. They were utilitarian only and she had no idea why they chose to ignore their given names. Was it a relinquishment or a renouncement, she wondered. She wanted to ask but could not do so. It seemed a very personal question and she didn't know these men well enough to ask it. She, instead, focused on the task at hand.

"How much longer before we can leave?"

"We should leave in fifteen minutes or so," Robert answered, still reluctant.

A look of concern crossed Einstein's face. He looked at Robert questioningly. "Exactly what is the course of action you intend to undertake?"

"We're going to make our way over to Adler's. He'll let me use the phone and let them stay there until someone can come and get them."

Einstein nodded his head. "I am aware of Adler's Pub and the forthrightness of the proprietor."

"If we leave here in another fifteen minutes or so, we should get there before eleven. I don't think Big Willie will close before then."

"Forgive me for questioning your judgment regarding such matters, Dogman," Einstein said uncomfortably, glancing over at Allison, "but I believe you might be underestimating the time such a trek would demand. Particularly, and forgive me for saying so, madam, with a woman and child in tow."

"I can't convince her to stay here while I go. Not that I blame her."

"Perhaps you've been out of the weather longer than I imagine but the snow has commenced once again. And may I say, it is an earnest storm. The reports are that another six to eight inches are expected with strong winds." Einstein turned to Allison. "Madam, I can understand your apprehension in staying in such a foul place as this any longer than is necessary. I fear that Dogman is correct in that you should remain here while he summons help. It is a night truly not fit for man or beast. You and your lovely daughter are in need of warmth and dryness and, although this place is undesirable, it offers both. It is also a place known by very few. I beg of you, remain here with myself and Yellow. He is a loyal and ever vigilant creature and you can be assured of your protection."

Although she was warmer now, the cold she experienced earlier stuck with her like a nightmare seconds after waking. The thought of entering back into it had never been enticing in the least but if it had meant getting Madison to the safety and comfort of her own bed and not staying any longer than necessary in this forsaken place, so be it. The situation had changed. Safety and comfort were not words she would choose but staying in this place with Einstein was certainly the lesser of two evils. She liked the man and she sensed that he was probably almost as savvy about their current situation as Robert. Even still, it was hard to suppress the urge to keep moving. She needed the sense of accomplishment. She needed to feel like she was doing something to get them out of this. Maintaining movement, at least temporarily, alleviated her sense of frustration, her helplessness. Allison was continually being humbled by decisions that did not come easily. Finally, the deciding factor was, of course, Madison. She watched her daughter now. Madison lay next to her with her head on Allison's thigh. She was not sleeping but was gently stroking the dog as it lay next to her with one of its paws also upon Allison's thigh. Forcing her daughter to put on wet shoes over wet socks and subjecting her to such weather was completely alien to her motherly instinct.

"All right," she sighed resignedly.

"A most prudent decision." The relief was evident upon Einstein's face. "Dogman, you should depart at once."

Robert had begun to prepare as soon as Allison had mouthed the words. Upon standing and readying himself to leave, Yellow jumped up, hoping to accompany her master. The dog had already forgotten about the snow and the discomfort the cold caused as it slowly moved up through the padding on her paws and permeated her body. Standing by the door, gently discouraging the dog from following, Robert gazed down at Allison intently. "You will be safe here. I'll be back as soon as I can and you'll be on your way home before you know it." As he made his way toward the door from which Einstein and the dog had entered, he looked at his friend with unspoken words.

Einstein gave him a small smile. "Be swift and be safe, my friend."

Robert acknowledged the send off with a wave just before the door swung closed.

CHAPTER TEN

10:37 p.m. Thursday

"Nobody's seen them since they were spotted at The Shamrock. That was about an hour and a half ago." Lonnie listened into the phone for a moment. "I don't know. Brick didn't say. But that's Callahan's place and we're not about to get any help from that prick." He listened for another moment. "Nobody seems to know where this guy stays. I've heard at least ten different places, most of which we checked out. I'm guessing most of them were bullshit. We found nothing. He seems to have only one friend he's ever been seen with, some guy they call Einstein, and nobody's seen him, either. The guy's a ghost right now." Lonnie was standing in the recess formed by the entrance to a two-story building, which had housed a paper products wholesaler before the business went under seven years ago. He had been looking out toward the street but the wind had turned and he had to force himself into the corner of the alcove just to hear Gerard on the other end of the line. "I haven't heard anything from him since he told me about The Shamrock." The elements and the connection made Gerard's voice hard to hear, even still, Lonnie had to pull the phone away from his ear to prevent his boss's yelling from damaging his eardrum. "Look, Martin, I can't say for sure that they're not gone but my gut tells me they're still here. We got reliable people all over within a radius of almost two miles of where they've been seen. With the weather the way it is, nobody's goin' too far too fast. And there sure aren't any vehicles making trips through here. So relax. We'll get this done."

After he hit the end button on the cell phone, he punched in Brick's number. Brick had no information other than the fact that he was about a mile from Lonnie's location. He then called Carson and had to roust him out of the warmth of some bar in which he was holed up. Lonnie shook his head in disgust. Brother-in-law of Gerard or not, his life line was growing shorter by the minute. It was hard for Lonnie to blame the big man, though. The warmth of some bar and some whiskey was certainly inviting. But if this job didn't get done, the only warmth they might see for the foreseeable future would be at the invitation of the state. The thought of incarceration was never far from his mind and, although it wasn't something he wanted, it didn't scare him. In fact, most times when he considered it, he could think of worse ideas than spending so much leisure time with so many men in such close proximity.

He exited the protection of the entryway, stretched the collar of his overcoat higher on his neck and trudged down the sidewalk through the again deepening snow. As he passed through the light spilling from the window of yet another open bar, he glanced inside to make certain one of their young guards was present. Lonnie didn't know the kid's name but he recognized the face. He guessed the kid was probably fifteen and should be home doing his geometry homework. It was getting difficult to keep track of them all. There were so many, so willing to work for Gerard. From time to time he felt sorry for them. Less often he felt responsible for their veering off course. Lonnie never wondered how kids at that age could feel that their lives were so hopeless that working for Gerard seemed like a way out. He had been one of them. The money Gerard paid them was more than they could earn at any of the menial jobs available to them. Jobs that were becoming more scarce and further away. School just wasn't an option. Even if they became inspired to excel, high school would be as far as the vast majority of them would get. Scholarships were even more scarce than the menial jobs and the colleges didn't trust the education dealt out at the inner city schools. Without a scholarship, a college education wasn't a dream but just pure whimsy. What does a kid do these days with nothing but a high school diploma? Not much, Lonnie knew, and they did too. Gerard offered them a chance to stand on their own, something no one else was doing despite what was said.

A couple of blocks further on Lonnie encountered two men huddled in a building entryway, trying to escape from the wind and snow that pelted their faces. He walked up the three stairs that led to the entrance and the two men cowered away from him.

"Relax, I'm not going to hurt you," Lonnie said in a voice that fought to be heard, "You two ever heard of some guy named Dogman?" He was still three feet from the two men and the wind howled through the small space but he could smell the stench that emanated from them. It was a familiar stench that was both powerful and sour. The bundles of tattered clothing they wore were unlaundered and surely reeked but that smell was overwhelmed by the odor of bodies long unwashed. Through the layers of rags that covered them he could see that they were barely more than animated skeletons. When neither responded to his question, he asked slowly and deliberately, "Have you seen a man with a woman and a child who don't look like they belong around here? The man goes by the name of Dogman."

One of the men spoke but it was barely more than a whisper. His voice quivered and his teeth chattered. "No, but we been tryin' real hard to find 'em. We really have."

Lonnie could see the other man nodding to emphasize his friend's statement. He got a good look at their faces then and he tried to look away but couldn't. Despite having seen it so many times before, it was mesmerizing. Their unshaven faces were sickly pale and emaciated. Staring at them from only three feet it was difficult to see their eyes that were sunken so far into their skulls. He shook himself free after a moment and turned to leave. As he stepped down out of the entryway, he knew these two would pay with their lives tonight in hopes of earning Gerard's reward money. He turned back toward them.

"Have you two got someplace warm to stay?"

"Well, yeah, it's okay, kinda. But we wanna find those people you talkin' about. That's alotta money."

"Look, I'll tell you what. How about if I give you some money and you guys go back to wherever it is you stay and don't come out until this storm passes?"

At the mention of money, life flowed back into the skeletons. The one who had spoken earlier spoke again. His voice was still a whisper but his teeth no longer chattered. "How much money?"

Lonnie started digging for his wallet. "I'll give you twenty apiece."

"Make it fifty and we'll go."

Angered at the attempt to negotiate a gift, Lonnie lunged toward the man with his fist pulled back. His intent was only to threaten. "Listen to me, old man. I was tryin' to do you a favor and this is how you treat me? You're gonna die out here if you stay much longer. Lotta good that two grand is gonna do you then, huh? How 'bout I don't give you anything and just put the two of you outta your misery right now?"

"Sorry," the man managed to mutter.

"Damn right you are." Lonnie finally pulled out his wallet and fished two twenties from it. "Now here's forty bucks. Go back to your place and stay there. If I see you out here again tonight, I'm gonna kill you myself, understand? And you don't say a word about this to anybody, got it? Now get outta here." Just after he let go of the bills, he said, "And use some of that money to take a goddamn bath."

Lonnie watched the two shuffle away huddled close together trying to ward off the cold and wind. He could almost work up a sadness for their plight but years of exposure to them had created a thin layer of callousness. He didn't worry that the money he had just given them would be put to good use. Most people with little knowledge of the homeless, knowledge that was gained only through the media, would assume that the two men Lonnie had just handed forty dollars to would immediately purchase liquor or some other vice. After all, their lack of knowledge let them believe that most of the homeless were so because of some form of addiction or weakness. He knew better. The two he had just met were typical examples of those that roamed the streets. Liquor was rarely the first thing on their minds. When the human body is without water, it thirsts for it. When it is without food, it hungers for it. It knows what it needs and that is what it will satisfy first, particularly when the need is as overwhelming as it is in the majority of these people. Seeing them so often, knowing a few of them personally, made Lonnie realize a long time ago how close he was, how close almost anyone is, to being in the same situation. Certainly bad choices could put you on the street but he knew more than a few who ended up there simply because of bad luck. No, he knew these two would find nourishment as soon as they could. Their bodies were racked with the indescribable pain of hunger and their bodies would accept nothing less. And though Lonnie hoped, chances were slim they would use the money to wash either themselves or their clothes.

After the two men disappeared around the corner, Lonnie continued on with his search. He glanced at his watch and saw that it was ten forty-five and started to worry that the bars might begin to close. They were the only places that remained open, the only places that had accessible phones for those without a place to stay. If the bars closed, whoever this guy was that had the women might just hideout for the night. That would make it next to impossible to find them before morning and there was no telling what the morning might bring. As long as the bars stayed open, there was something to attract them. Like moths to a flame.

Exiting the building that served as their latest haven, the snow was falling heavily and the wind was whipping. Robert instinctively glanced behind him to make sure Yellow was with him before he realized that he had left her behind. It was unusual that they weren't together. Today was the first time in a long while that he was on the streets without her. Einstein had somehow scored some actual dog food and there was no dragging her away from it. The fact that she wasn't with him now and the curiosity that Madison had shown earlier caused him to think about the day Yellow entered his life. The dog had attached herself to him when he had first hit the streets, almost two years ago now.

The MGM Casino in downtown Lordmont loomed ahead like a beacon, crying out to those in need of hope. As Robert made his way from the parking structure toward the casino, he patted his wallet that held his last two hundred dollars. He knew the casino was not really the answer. Still, there was some hope that he could get lucky and turn the two hundred into something more substantial. But how substantial could it possibly be? And how could it possibly rescue him from where he was? Even if he won something, he still had no source of reliable income. Soon, he'd run through his winnings and he'd be back where he was. What were the chances he could win a substantial amount every time he needed it? He had no viable way of making income. Jobs in the state were becoming nonexistent. Interviews were even becoming scarce. He never did finish his degree and, despite being a veteran, being a partner in a failed real estate company did not exactly endear himself to potential employers.

While he cautiously hoped that he could turn the two hundred into something more, he was also going to the casino to feel more a part of life. Not having worked for four months (it might have been more but he didn't want to count) and being without a fiancee, he had been isolated. He hoped that being out among people would make him matter.

Entering the casino through the bank of revolving doors, he had to look at a woman twice to make certain that it wasn't Karen. Despite being relieved that it was not, she occupied his mind, as she did so often lately. It not only still amazed him how quickly she had turned on him when his source of income had dried up, it was frightening in its completeness. It was nothing short of mental castration. Despite his diligence in search of employment, her interest in him seemed to wane rapidly. When he would talk about the potential of this job or that, she feigned interest poorly. After a time, he came to realize that his position as a partner in a real estate venture was much more becoming to her than the possibility of him being employed as a middle manager or manager trainee in some innocuous company. He had to admit that he felt the same way but weren't they a team? It pained him to think that she would suffer embarrassment that her betrothed was not something of which she could be proud. She rectified that situation a few weeks back when she departed for her family's home on the west side of the state and cut off all communications with him.

Despite calling her parents' home twice, she had never returned his calls. Apparently, in her mind, the terse note she had left on the bed in their apartment was sufficient. He'd never had the chance to ask her if she could, perhaps, give him his fair share of the savings that she had built up in her own name while he paid the rent. He thought they were saving it for their future. He misunderstood that she was saving it for hers. Much like Tommy Abernathy, his former business partner, she had suckered him, too.

As expected, the casino proved fruitless. At the blackjack tables, he had built the two hundred up to three-fifty over the course of a couple of hours, but in less than forty-five minutes with an unconsciously hot dealer, he was back to fifty bucks. It was then that the gravity of the situation, once again, slammed him hard. The realism of it made him nauseous and he would have lost it right there at the table if the rest of his body didn't prefer passing out. He somehow managed to fight it off and made his way out of the casino.

He had tried not to think about the end of his resources being near at hand. He had figured that something would have to come up. Afterall, he wasn't a loser. He wasn't lazy, he wasn't an addict. Yet, he had fifty bucks to his name. He was months behind on his rent and the refrigerator and his balance sheet were empty. There was actually nothing, absolutely nothing, that was going to fix this.

Now, he wanted only to get back to his apartment, get some sleep and try to figure it all out again in the morning. The blood was making its way back to his face and extremities but he still felt as if he weren't in the present. He struggled to remember where he had parked and staggered through the parking structure. He thought he heard something behind him but couldn't be certain in his current state. After that, there was nothing.

Something was licking his face. When he was first aware of the sensation, he thought he was dreaming. Ever so slowly the devastating pounding that assaulted his head brought him out of his slumber and made him realize that he wasn't dreaming. Something was actually licking his face. He flailed his arms at the intrusion and hit something solid that made noise in response. *The licking stopped. He opened his eyes and sat up. The pain was enough to make focus difficult. After a moment he was able to finally make out his surroundings. He was in a corner of the parking structure against the cement walls near the stairs and the dim gray light of the spring dawn was penetrating between the first and second tiers. He put his hands to his head and closed his eyes in an attempt to stave off the pain and the pounding but it provided little relief. After a moment he remembered the licking and opened his eyes once again. Standing three feet away from him was a dog with a yellow-brown coat of matted fur, staring at him and wagging its tail. Instead of wondering why he was sitting on the floor of the parking structure with a throbbing headache worse than he had ever felt, he was more curious as to why there was a dog there.*

He stared at the dog in wonderment for a few seconds. Then reality relentlessly seeped back into him and he lost interest in the animal. He gingerly touched the knot on the back of his head. Instinctively, he felt for his wallet. It was gone from his back pocket. He frantically searched the other pockets of his pants and jacket. It wasn't anywhere. Not only that, there wasn't anything in any of his pockets. No keys. Not to his car. Not to his apartment.

He rose from where he sat and had to steady himself by putting a hand to the wall. That lasted only a moment and he went back to his knees. He knelt for awhile until he was fairly certain he could stand. He waited a few more moments before moving about. He needed to convince himself that what he thought had happened actually had. When he came to the empty space where he knew he had parked, he knew the truth. Not only had he been robbed of the only money he had to his name, but he no longer had any transportation. The weight of it made his knees buckle and the nausea return. He avoided going down by supporting himself against a cement post nearby but he failed in his attempt to fight off the discomfort in his stomach.

When he recovered from purging what little there was in his stomach, he stood up, snuffed his nose and wiped the tears from his eyes. He looked around wondering what he was going to do and muttered, "What the fuck?"

He noticed movement toward the ground near him and looked downward. There was the dog with the yellow-brown coat of matted fur sniffing his vomit. With so little undigested food in it, it was unattractive even to the dog. The dog looked up at him, wagging its tail once again.

The lights still burned in Adler's Pub at five minutes past eleven. They were a welcome sight and instilled hope in Robert. The frightful weather had made the journey arduous. Another inch and a half of snow had fallen during his trek and the wind wanted to create snowblindness. Despite the delay it had caused, it was to his benefit. Even if the streets hadn't been deserted he would have been difficult to spot. When he pressed the metal latch on the door, the wind wrenched it from his hand and blew it open, slamming it against the wall. Most of the twenty or so patrons turned to look. Robert closed it behind him and shook the snow from his clothing. He gazed around the bar. Chances were slim that he would recognize any of Gerard's men. Besides, he knew there were many others who had joined the hunt, having been lured by the reward and a chance to do the man a favor. Having the aegis of a man like Gerard in this part of the city was more than enough reward. Robert was simply scanning to see if anyone reacted more oddly than usual to the entrance of a homeless man.

He spied Big Willie at a table by the far wall with his back to him, apparently so engrossed in a newspaper that he had been the only one not to hear Robert enter the bar. As he approached, a young man that had been working behind the bar came toward him. He paid no attention to the bartender, intending to go directly to the far end to see Willie.

"Hey, you," the young man called out. Startled, Robert jerked his head around, poised for action, if necessary. "We don't allow your kind in here. You gotta leave."

"I just need to…" Robert uttered before being cut off.

"Now! Get outta here. Go back to your box." The bartender was nearing him.

Robert had been here before. He couldn't see the faces of the people behind him but he knew they were smirking in anticipation. They were waiting to see him forcibly thrown out of the bar, but hopefully not before some violence was visited upon him. He held up his hands in surrender. "Look…"

Willie's voice boomed throughout the room. "Dogman, how the hell ya doin'? Richard, leave the man alone. He's okay. Come on over here, Dogman."

Robert walked past the two pool tables to where Willie was seated. They shook hands and, as always, Robert's almost broke from the pressure of the man's grip.

"What the hell brings you out on such a night? I certainly wouldn't be if I didn't have to. But I got to 'cause that idiot nephew o' mine couldn't keep the place runnin' by hisself. That's him, who you just met. That mutt o' yers outside?"

"No, the dog's somewhere else. I need a favor, Willie."

"No shit? Happy to help. What can I do?"

"I need to use your phone."

"My phone? You came out on a night like this just to use my phone? Must be a pretty 'portant call. But I got bad news for ya, ol' buddy, I ain't got a phone here no more."

Robert's mouth dropped open. He had finally found a place Gerard didn't have covered and it did him no good. "How could you not have a phone?" Robert asked incredulously.

"Things been a little tight lately and I couldn't afford it no more. Actually, it works out pretty good this way. Shelly can't call me no more and bitch for me to come home. And my customers don't get no more calls from their wives, neither. If I gotta order stuff, I jes do it from home. What d'ya need to make a call for, anyway?"

"How far do you live from here?"

"What? A coupla blocks. Why?"

"Can I use the phone at your house?" Robert noticed the desperation in his own voice. "Sorry, Willie. I know it's a big imposition but I really need to make a call."

"Who you gotta call so bad?"

Robert was convinced that Willie knew nothing of his predicament, which is precisely why he had thought of Adler's. It was far enough away from Gerard's territory that word hadn't spread this far. Yet. He had known Willie for close to two years, had done some odd jobs for him, and Robert was fairly confident that he could call him a friend. But he had seen the influence Gerard had on people. He wanted to trust him but there was just too much at stake. "I can't tell you that. I'm sorry. But I really need you to do this for me. I'll owe you big time."

Willie looked at him thoughtfully. He glanced toward the pool table and then back at Robert. "Maybe you won't have to owe me. I'll tell ya what. If you do me a favor right now, I'll let ya use the phone at my house."

"I'm in kind of hurry, Willie."

"This won't take long. See that young fella over there hittin' balls around?" He waited until Robert saw the young man. "He thinks he's a player and I'm willin' to bet that no matter how good I tell 'im you are, he'll still play ya."

"Willie, I really don't have time…"

"You wanna use my phone don't ya?" Willie looked at him hard, then softened. "Come on, Dogman. It won't take hardly any time at all."

Robert didn't seem to have a choice. He had nowhere else to go. It might go quickly. And if he could score some cash, he could take something to eat back to the women. They hadn't eaten but some crackers since this afternoon. Reluctantly, he finally nodded at Willie. "All right, but just one game."

"Hey, George. Come over here."

The young man sauntered over to join them. Robert surmised that he was no more than twenty-five years old. He was short, maybe five-six or five-seven, and rail thin. The look in his eyes said he wasn't to be screwed with.

"George, this guy here's name's Dogman. He's one of the best players I ever seen. Even better than you." Robert shook his head. George looked him up and down and couldn't imagine how someone dressed such as Robert could possibly play pool better than himself. "I'm telling you this," Big Willie continued, "because I don't want you to come cryin' to me afterward, tellin' me that you was set up. Okay? How 'bout it? You wanna play 'im for somethin'?"

"How much?" George asked. The tone of the question made it

clear that George wasn't concerned about the amount. Rather, it was an indication of how good the opponent was. Usually, the larger the bet, the better the player.

"How 'bout fifty and you git the break?"

Robert gave Willie a frown. He hated it when Willie gave them the break. "Oh, that's smart," he said under his breath.

George smiled and let out a derisive snort. "Fine," he said with mild disinterest and went to the table.

Willie winked at Robert. "Let's hope he don't make the eight on the snap. The usual?"

Robert nodded at him. The usual meant that Willie covered the losses and the winnings were split evenly. This was one of the odd jobs that Robert did for him from time to time. One night, almost two years ago, Robert had wandered into Adler's and before Willie could throw him out, Robert had actually paid for a drink. As he was a paying customer, Willie had let him stay. When they ended up on the pool table, Willie discovered the extent of Robert's talent. That night, Willie asked Robert if he had any money and did he want to play. Robert gave Willie much the same warning that Willie had just given George. For awhile after that it had become a routine for them. Willie always warned the opponent that they were going to lose, yet they were rarely at a loss for an opponent. At first Robert had enjoyed it. It beat the boredom and provided him with some cash. It didn't hurt that he was risking nothing. But it was a routine borne of success. The first time he lost, he had not played particularly well and Willie let him know it. But Willie didn't stop there and added some other comments to which Robert took offense. Although Willie later apologized for his comments, things were never the same. Robert grew tired of the partnership. He never mentioned it to Willie, but Robert had begun to feel somewhat like a sideshow, like a monkey to Willie's organ grinding. Here he was again, but this time it was with good reason.

He racked the colored balls and prayed that George didn't sink the eight on the break. The cue ball smacked the triangular rack and, as the balls caromed around the table, Robert wondered if Willie would be so willing to let him use the phone if he lost. Not one ball managed to find a pocket and Robert stood to survey the table. There were three striped balls sitting close to two end rail pockets and one side pocket. They were easily made. After that, pocketing the other four would involve difficult positional play because their paths to the most logical pockets were blocked by solid-colored balls. As the balls lay now, there was only one makeable solid. Five other solids had their paths blocked by striped balls. The last solid lay frozen against the eight ball near one of the end rails. Robert envisioned the entire game in his head before it even played out. He would sink the one solid that was now makeable and then purposely miss his next shot, being careful not to disturb the rest of the table. George, being left with stripes, would have no choice but to pocket the open shots, clearing paths for Robert's balls. Being out of makeable shots, George would then, in all likelihood, miss and Robert would have an open table. The strategy generally worked, it was simply a matter of odds. The reason it usually worked was because the person who first begins clearing their balls from the table would find it increasingly difficult. As their balls dwindle, so do the available shots because the other person's balls still clutter the table. Once that person misses, the second player has a much less difficult time because the table is now clear of all but one or two of the opponent's balls.

The only thing wrong with Robert's strategy was that George was a better player than expected. George found ways to make the cue ball dance around the table, breaking free the stripes that were originally blocked. Before the eight ball was freed from the spot where it lay frozen to one of the solids, though, the cue ball ceased dancing. George attempted a nearly impossible shot, which only freed up Robert's solid and left the eight ball rolling harmlessly around the table nowhere near the called pocket. The common ailment of the typical bar player, Robert noted to himself, was their inability to play safe, a concept with which they were unfamiliar. For the atypical player familiar with the concept, more often than not they were simply unwilling. When he stepped to the table, the balls, which were all his solids and the eight ball, were well spaced and easily runnable. Just as he bent down to take the first shot, *Riding the Storm Out* by REO Speedwagon came on the juke box. The song was apropos for the current weather and the customers in the bar howled with delight, but it took Robert away from the present for a few moments. He tapped his foot to the music and there was a bounce to his walk as he made his way around the table sinking balls. He even managed to play a few air guitar riffs on the pool cue. As the song ended, he returned to the present, took a large breath that ended in a sigh, bent down, and pocketed the eight ball.

When he looked up from the table, Willie was just exiting his office. "Yeah, that's what I'm talkin' 'bout," Willie exclaimed.

After George paid off the bet, Willie handed the entire amount to Robert. "Why don't ya' keep all of it." In response to Robert's questioning look, he said, "I feel kinda bad 'bout how we ended up a few months back. This is my way of makin' up. Besides, you could use it more than me, right?" After a short hesitation of silence, he added, "C'mon, my coat's in the office. We can go out the back."

Willie's reasoning for handing over the entire amount did nothing to dissolve the questioning look on Robert's face. Big Willie's behavior was strangely subdued, which was unusual for him, particularly after having won the bet. Robert finally brushed it off. He had other concerns at the moment and he was about to get to a phone.

Robert cooled his heels impatiently while Willie talked with his nephew behind the bar for a few minutes. In the office, Robert fidgeted in the chair fronting the desk as Willie rifled through the drawers. Although Robert heard the office door open behind him, he didn't turn around until the door closed and the locked was engaged. He knew something was wrong and stood up immediately. He eyed the door at the back of the office, but not in an inconspicuous way, and that is when the gun appeared.

"This is my cousin, Brick. I'm really sorry 'bout this, Dogman. He jes wants to know where they are."

CHAPTER ELEVEN

11:18 p.m. Thursday

He was lost. Certainly figuratively, possibly physically. The ceaseless whipping snow he had endured for the past hour and a half combined with the endless white and identical buildings block after block was leaving him dazed. The people he encountered on the streets were few, and that number was dwindling. Those he had spoken to knew nothing or chose not reveal anything that might cost them a shot at the reward.

Cops are confident people by nature and John Draganchuk was no different. To augment that confidence, they were trained to prepare for most circumstances. While their nature and training served them well, from time to time it created self-assuredness that lacked substance. It was this feeling Draganchuk was fighting at the moment. He was not prepared for what he was now experiencing. It wasn't that he was cold, although that was certainly part of it. He had underestimated the weather and should have dressed differently. It wasn't that he was a suburban cop in the big city. Afterall, he had spent enough time here to know that he could blend in with the crowds and go unnoticed if need be. The problem was there were no crowds within which to blend. The snow had driven almost everyone into their homes. The only people who weren't driven to their homes were either those without one or those who preferred a bar, the only establishments that remained open after the storm hit. Earlier, when he had entered the first bar he came across, it became crystal clear that he would not go unnoticed. The bars were filled with few customers, all of which were very local due to the impossible driving conditions. Unknown to anyone, he was immediately regarded with suspicion. Thus, he was relegated to the streets, stealing temporary refuge whenever he could from recessed doorways.

Though he had little experience with the people of the street, he tried to act the part by shuffling his feet, a difficult task for certain in deep snow, hunching his shoulders and taking on a wary aura when people were nearby. He encountered a woman not long after leaving that first bar and knew however hard he may try, he could not imitate the persona. The wind and snow may disguise his walk or his posture, possibly even his clothes, but nothing Draganchuk might do could possibly replicate that haggard and hollow look known only to those people in that condition.

Draganchuk looked furtively around the next corner and then peered at his watch. It was nearing eleven-thirty and his frustration was peaking. There was no way of finding out what was going on. He felt powerless and was considering calling off his search. He decided he'd give it another half-hour or so, then stop in a bar, not care who thought what, make a couple of calls and head for his car. He wanted to come to the aid of his friend but he doubted anymore he had the capability to do so. Up ahead a half a block a man was trudging through the snow. Draganchuk hunched his shoulders and began shuffling toward the man.

As the policeman neared, the other man called out to him, "Hey, how ya doin'?"

He didn't feel like yelling through the wind, so Draganchuk said nothing and kept walking toward him. The other man stopped walking forward when he got no response. Draganchuk took notice of the other man's wariness and, not wanting to scare him off, he yelled back, "Okay, how 'bout you?"

"I could use somethin' to get the cold outta me. You got anything?"

"No, man. I got nothin'. I was hopin' you did." Draganchuk's antennae were up. This guy's demeanor said he knew the streets.

"Shit, man. Ain't we a sight. Worst goddamn snow storm in history and we got no party favors."

"Life, she is a bitch."

"Ya got that right."

They stood in silence for a moment with their backs to the wind. Draganchuk watched the man out of the corner of his eye move from side to side. He noted the ceaseless movement of an addict. He bided his time waiting for the other man to talk, trying not to appear anxious to extend the conversation. After a time when the man said nothing, he thought screw this. It was too cold and time was wasting. If he spooked the guy, he'd be the bad cop and threaten him for information.

"My name's John. Who are you?" Might as well be blunt.

"Two Spoon," the other man answered without hesitation. "What're ya out on such a night for? Jes tryin' to score somethin'?"

Draganchuk decided he was a gregarious guy. It suited his addiction. He plunged ahead. "Always, my man, always. But words out y'know? Lookin' for a guy named Dogman. Gonna try 'n score some o' that reward money. Know what I'm sayin'?"

"I do. Think I might be gettin' some of it, too, 'cause I saw the guy earlier tonight. Told Brick 'bout it, too."

Damn, thought Draganchuk, maybe they already found them. "Who's Brick?"

"You don't know Brick? I thought everybody knew 'im. He's one o' Gerard's top guys."

"So, what, they got the guy?"

"Nah. I jes saw Lonnie not too long ago. The guy's like disappeared. Nobody knows where he is."

Relief washed through him and then an idea struck him. "Sorry 'bout the reward money, man, but I'll tell ya what. I gotta deal for ya."

Two Spoon's eyes lit up. He was always in the mood for a deal. "What's that?"

"I know exactly where they're at."

"No shit? Where, man?"

"That's privileged information, my man. But here's the deal. I don't know what Lonnie or Brick looks like or where they're at. So you take me to 'em and I'll split the reward with ya."

Two Spoon thought it was too good to be true. All he had to do was take him to Lonnie or Brick? Was this guy stupid or what? "No problem, man. I can do that. We split fifty-fifty, right? I get a grand, right?"

"That's right. We're a team, my man."

Yeah, right, Two Spoon thought to himself. "C'mon man. I saw Lonnie this way." It was too good to be true but maybe it could get better. Two Spoon could never help himself. "Ya know, with this weather the way it is 'n all, we might get split up. If that happens and I find Lonnie without ya, I won't be able to tell 'im nothin' if ya don't tell me. Ya know I'll split the reward money with ya. Two Spoon is a man o' his word."

For a time after Dogman had left, the two females and Einstein were silent. Madison had fallen asleep with Yellow by her side. The dog only drifted in and out of slumber, awakening occasionally to the woeful sounds of the sewer lines that ran throughout the building. Allison had kept a watchful eye on her new host. Earlier he had rooted around in his back pack and pulled from it a letter-sized note pad filled with pages that were worn and dog-eared. For some time now he had been writing in the pad with a pencil no more than three inches long.

"It's none of my business but I'm curious. What is that you're writing?" Allison asked softly.

He smiled gently. "I am somewhat chagrined to admit that it is a diary of a sort. Or more aptly put, the musings of an old man."

"Do you enjoy writing?"

"What is scribbled here can hardly be characterized as writing. Writing is an art, which takes a talent that I lack. What I have entered on these pages are simply observations. They are deficient in structure and coherent thought."

She laughed quietly. "I sincerely doubt that. What do you observe? And why?"

"My surroundings. My daily life and the people I encounter. I find it has therapeutic value on more than one level. As you may have guessed, a man in my position has a great deal of leisure time. Not that I am complaining, mind you, but as with so many things, too much of anything can make it less desirable. I have discovered that committing to paper what I see and what I do is a valuable use of time. Furthermore, it allows me to relieve any frustrations I may have regarding certain situations or individuals."

Allison looked at him curiously.

"Your expression indicates that you are not satisfied with my explanation."

"It just seems to me that people who choose to keep a diary do it for another purpose. A young girl keeps a diary to look at when she's older. Adults keep journals to track an experiment, or to hand down to their children, or even to write an autobiography."

It was Einstein's turn to smile at her. "You are not without perception, Madam. You have forced me to expose my true purpose. I am uncomfortable in admitting, as heretofore I have admitted this to only one other person, that my aspirations are for these observations to fall into those hands that might make use of them. You see, I am one individual within a quite extraordinary amassment of people that exists like no other grouping. What I find so interesting is that, at least on the surface, the other groupings within our society find no interest whatsoever in another subset of their own species. And because there is such a lack of interest, their size is underestimated, and their thoughts and opinions are ignored. A society such as ours that chooses to disregard such a large part of its makeup is a true phenomenon.

"But please, do not misinterpret what I say. I am not an advocate. I certainly believe that valuable thoughts and opinions can come from this sector of our society, however, it would demand someone much more scholarly than I to determine how to assimilate such information. My self-appointed task is to simply observe and record my thoughts as they pertain to this segment of our society from a vantage point that is most beneficial. These insights, if I may be so presumptuous as to call them such, will, hopefully, someday allow a clearer understanding of the persons that exist in this part of our society."

When he finally finished, Allison was simply staring at him, continuing to smile.

"I am sorry. I've once again caused an onslaught of ennui. As I said earlier, rhetoric is a weakness of mine."

"No. No, that's quite all right. I enjoy listening to you very much. I was quiet only because I was trying to catch up with you."

Silence fell over them once again. Allison watched her daughter for the moment and patted the dog. Yellow looked up at her briefly, glanced around the room and then lay her head back down. Einstein moved the pencil across the paper. Although sleep had visited her earlier, it did not now. She sensed that she was closer to rescue now that Robert was able to move about freely. That thought kept her wide awake. She was having difficulty with the quiet.

"Can you tell me about Robert?"

"What would you like to know?"

She struggled with her question. Somehow it seemed inappropriate and she had been trying hard all day not to be. "Where...where did he come from? How did he end up here? It doesn't...he..."

His gentle smile returned. It was a patient and fatherly smile. "He doesn't appear to belong here?"

She felt her cheeks flush now that the question was aired. "Neither of you do. I guess I'm a very sheltered person."

"Nonsense. There are many things about your existence that I do not comprehend, as well."

She doubted it but chose not to voice it.

"You are correct, though. Dogman is different than the typical denizen. It is, perhaps, because he was in the game much longer than most of us. He certainly participated at a higher level. Perhaps more so, I think, he more or less chose to live here." With that revelation, a questioning look appeared on Allison's face. "You find that quite astonishing, do you not?" She nodded. "Believe it or not," he continued quietly, "there are those who have actually chosen this way of life. Granted, there are not many but there are more than you might think."

"Why would he choose it?"

Einstein gazed at one of the candles for a few seconds, massaging the tight salt and pepper curls of his beard. His deep brown eyes did not move from the light, as if the answer she sought lay within the flame. "I believe it was for myriad reasons, as should be necessary in order to undertake such an extraordinary change in one's life. I do not know the extent of those reasons, and what I do know, I know only from what he has told me. This particular chapter began when the economy of our state began its horrid and seemingly bottomless descent. Dogman, you see, was heavily invested in real estate. Apparently, so heavily invested and so certain that his success would march on uninterrupted that he did not provide for himself a safety net. A rainy day fund, if you will. Most unfortunately, for Dogman, as for so many of the general populace, that rainy day presented itself and the rain has yet to cease. As I am sure you are aware, jobs and even business enterprises began to disappear from the state, resulting in a mass exodus of tenants from his buildings. I am led to understand that from that point forward the unpleasantness of the situation grew to epic proportions. In no time at all rent collections became insufficient to satisfy mortgage payments and property taxes. Not long after this calamity, the impatience of the mortgage holders reached its limit and the foreclosures began.

"Now, according to our Dogman, he entreated those with whom he had debt to willingly adjust their needs and found some success. His hope was that the economy would stop its plummet and begin to recover. His tenants would then return and he could, once again, satisfy his obligations. However, no one could estimate the depth to which this economy would fall and Dogman never had the opportunity to fulfill his agreements. Finally, he yielded to what seemed destined and walked away."

When Einstein finally paused to take a breath, Allison spoke before he could continue. "How could he just walk away from his obligations? Why didn't he just sell his properties to pay off the mortgages?"

Einstein studied her for a moment. It was obvious by her tone of voice that she was not only disappointed in Dogman, she was insulted that he could feel justified in simply walking away from his obligations. Einstein was familiar with many whom had run up against odds that were insurmountable in the truest sense of the word. There's not always an answer and if there's nowhere to go, there's nowhere to go. Allison's disappointment with his friend would not go undefended.

"I must apologize to you. It is my inability to fully explain Dogman's position that has caused you to misunderstand his actions." He continued to hold her gaze to make certain she understood what he had just said. His defense of his friend was not in his tone of voice, which remained even. It was in his eyes and Allison saw it. "As you may or may not have heard, the seriousness of the illness within which our economy finds itself is such that real estate prices declined severely. So severe, in fact, that in many cases the perceived value of property was less than the amount for which it was financed. As you have suggested, he did attempt to sell his properties but found no success. Apparently, offers he did receive from anyone remotely interested were laughable. In his words, not mine, he was not going to allow them to profit from his misery. Dogman convinced himself that walking away was the only choice. As you might imagine, I have been privy to many unhappy tales in my time. I cannot begin to say to you that I understand the business Dogman was in, but I have been convinced over the years that walking away is, sometimes, not just the best but the only alternative."

Despite the unfairness, Allison still could not comprehend how Robert could just choose to drop out. "That's certainly a sad story but why couldn't he just start over? A person can always find a job. A fast food restaurant or a department store, some place like that."

"I don't know the answer to that. I have never queried and he has never volunteered. I should further inform you that there are a couple more pieces to the story. Perhaps, these matters will help you better understand his state of mind. There was a partner in his business. For whatever reasons, Dogman was the one who provided funds whenever necessary. When the business began to founder, his partner refused to provide any of his own funds and, in fact, left the state and left Dogman to clean up the mess. Also at the time, Dogman was engaged to a woman he had known for three years. She, too, left when she saw trouble on the horizon.

"So, can I tell you why he has chosen not to start over? No. I suppose that he could have taken a position at a fast food restaurant, as you have suggested. I suspect, however, that it is a difficult proposition for a person who has achieved a high level of success to do such a thing. I would think that losing everything is much like a death in that one would have to make their way through the five steps before acceptance of the inevitable. But he lost a business, and a friend, and a lover. And these things were taken from him not necessarily because of decisions he made or actions he took but simply because of the whims of the economy, not unlike losing everything in a tempest. But when you lose everything in a storm, your friends and lovers don't leave. I believe our Dogman is here because he is still working through the steps and has not yet achieved acceptance."

Neither one spoke for awhile after that. After several minutes, Allison was overtaken by exhaustion despite their rescue being imminent. She lay down next to Madison, causing the girl to stir. Her daughter opened her eyes and whispered, "I wake up sometimes and hear you guys talking."

"Uh huh," Allison whispered back.

"I don't understand most of the things he says."

CHAPTER TWELVE

11:31 p.m. Thursday

They had never met but Dogman needed no introduction. Even if he hadn't glimpsed him from time to time around this desolate area of the city they shared, he would have known this person to be Brick. His herculean stature, his beard of gnarly black curls and the clean shaven skull made it impossible even for the most eremitic of local citizens not to recognize him. He had always found it interesting that even though most people knew who Brick was and for whom he worked, they looked upon him with as much respect as they did fear. Certainly, he was Gerard's enforcer but he was frugal, almost discriminating, in how he chose to administer his retribution. Word was that Brick seemed to have a sixth sense that enabled him to discern between extenuating circumstances and true bullshit. Recognizing the extenuating circumstances gained him the respect of the locals, recognizing the true bullshit and acting upon it swiftly and ruthlessly gained him Gerard's respect. In this area of the city, where the sight of an enforcer of a crime boss was not unusual, the fact that he was fair gained him acceptance as a member of the community. Dogman had heard how others spoke of Brick and, though Brick didn't know it nor had any reason to consider it, a seat on the city council representing this burnt out area of Lordmont was not out of reach.

Dogman had done his best to remain a stranger to Brick but, apparently, that was no longer the case. Although the gun was pointed directly at him, he noticed that Brick held it lazily, like someone who was very comfortable holding such a thing and aiming it at another person. By the same token, Dogman looked at the gun and felt very little. Despite the imminent danger, he found his lack of panic curious. A few years back, in the height of his real estate career, he suspected that seeing a gun pointed at him would have caused him to lose control of his bodily functions. Why he felt so little now he wasn't certain. Was it because he had seen the worst life could dole out over the last two or so years? Had he become callous? Or was it because he had so little to lose now and cared less about life? He made a mental note to consider this later.

Brick was the first to speak. "So, come with it. Where are they?"

Dogman turned to Big Willie and held his gaze long enough for Willie to finally look away. Then he shifted his gaze back to Brick. "I could tell you where they are, but it wouldn't do you much good." Dogman crossed his arms and leaned against the wall. His calmness was surprising to everyone in the room. "Even if I tried to tell you where they are, you'd have a hard time finding it. And if I'm not back in a reasonable amount of time, the person they're with will get them moving again."

"And who's that?" Brick asked.

Dogman simply stared at him and said nothing.

"And what's to stop me from just shooting you right now and finding them myself?"

"Nothing," Dogman responded, maintaining his composure. "But without me you've got no idea where to find them. And they're hidden well enough that it'll be well past daylight before you do. And that's if you find them. And with the daylight comes all sorts of possibilities."

Brick quietly stared at Dogman for a moment considering the next step. He slowly walked over to him. He stood very close to him, their noses almost touching. "So, you're ready to die for these people, people you don't even know?" Before a response could come, Brick drove his right fist into Dogman's stomach. Brick held him up for a few seconds and then let him slump to the floor. After several more seconds, Brick asked, again, "Are you ready to die for these people?"

Dogman struggled to a sitting position, gritting his teeth and working hard to suck wind back into his lungs. With his back to the wall, he massaged his aching stomach. Without looking up he said through a jaw that was clenched hard, "All right, I'll take you to them."

Brick squatted down letting the gun dangle in his hand near Dogman's face. "No. You tell me where they are."

He needed the time on the street. Besides, he knew if he parted with the information, he was of no use to Brick. "It's impossible to get to if you don't know where you're going. Not only that, they'll know you're coming before you get close."

The two men looked at each other for a few moments. Finally, Brick let out a sigh. He tapped the top of Dogman's head with the barrel of the gun and rose to his feet. "Okay, *Dawgman*," Brick said sardonically, "You bought yourself some time. Let's go."

Just before he exited in front of Brick, Dogman turned back to his traitorous friend. "Bye, Willie."

Outside on the streets, the gusting wind savagely buffeted their bodies, driving them backward if they didn't lean into it. When the frenzied blowing would cease abruptly they would tumble forward. It was difficult enough to move in the ever-deepening snow that now measured beyond seventeen inches; the wind made it near impossible. The wind chill plummeted with each gust and Dogman secured his stocking cap and shoved his gloved hands deep into the pockets of his long coat. Brick wore only a small watch cap to cover his head and he stretched it to the limit in an attempt to cover as much of his ears and forehead as he could. He turned up the collar of his waist-length leather coat and hunched his shoulders in order to cover his neck and face. He swore quietly, knowing too much skin was exposed to the elements.

Dogman had the advantage. He knew this just by looking at his escort. He was certainly no outdoorsman. Earlier in his life he hadn't hunted and rarely camped. Despite this, and somewhat unexpectedly based on how the two men chose to live their lives, for the conditions, he was the more appropriately dressed. He smiled to himself wondering how long ago, if ever, he had been able to think such a thing. He was also confident that he knew his way around better than Brick. Not that Brick was unfamiliar with the area. Dogman was certain the man knew the streets and could easily get from point A to point B. But no one knew this vicinity like he did. Dogman knew the buildings and alleyways. He knew which structures were completely abandoned and if they were safe and how to get through them. He also knew how to negotiate the unsafe ones. They had at least a thirty-minute trek ahead of them and Dogman was leading. He was more convinced now than when he was in the back room of Adler's Pub that there would be ample opportunity for him to separate himself from Brick.

Twenty minutes later Brick screamed through the wind, "Stop, now!"

Dogman ceased his monotonous trudging and waited for his captor to close the space between them. It was only twenty feet but the weather lengthened it considerably. Dogman watched the man make his way slowly toward him. The street they were now on was devoid of the wind. Dogman wasn't sure if the wind had begun to die or was blocked by the adjacent building. Still, the snow and cold made walking treacherous and it took Brick several seconds to close the gap. Although, at the moment, the man held Dogman's life in his hands, he couldn't help but feel some empathy for Brick. The endless pelting of snow had encrusted anything on the man that wasn't smooth. His navy blue watch cap was almost completely white, as were his eyebrows, mustache and most of his beard. Dogman studied the rest of his clothing and knew Brick wasn't long for the weather. While his leather coat blocked the gusts of wind and snow from reaching his body, the lack of insulation inside the leather allowed the dangerously low temperatures to penetrate. As Brick brought his feet up to almost knee height in order to take a step forward through the snow, he saw his boots. They were made of rubber with metal buckles and designed only to keep his feet dry. Dogman surmised that the man's toes were long past numb.

When Brick finally caught up, Dogman leaned close to him.

"We've still got a ways to go and you aren't going to make it dressed like that. We need to find you some shelter."

"Thanks for your concern," he replied sarcastically, "Don't worry about me and keep moving."

Dogman gazed at him. He tried not to stare at the snot that was creating an ever-increasing clot on his mustache. He shifted his gaze to his lips and saw them trembling, and he thought they might be purple but the lack of light made it difficult to be sure. He finally fixed on Brick's eyes and saw the dread in them. Brick tried to stare back intently and create an aura of control but it wasn't working. He knew the discomfort he was feeling now wasn't going to end any time soon. And it was such a great amount of discomfort, discomfort that could inflict injury, without any relief in sight, that panic began to nip at the edges of his mind. Though he tried, Dogman could not help but feel for the man. Who knows, maybe if he helped him it might make things easier. At any rate, maybe he could cause a delay.

"Look, the weather's going to make this trip longer than I thought." So was the indirect route on which he was leading them. "I'm willing to bet your toes and ears are already numb and you're fingers aren't far behind. If you don't get out of the snow before your clothes are soaked clear through, you're fucked. I suggest we bust down the door to that convenience store over there and find some heat."

Brick glanced across the street at the store and then back at Dogman. The enticement of heat was strong. He motioned the gun in the direction of the store and said, "Move."

After several attempts with the butt end of the weapon, the glass of the entrance door finally gave way. Neither man expected to hear an alarm go off, thus, they weren't surprised by the silence that followed the shattering glass. It wasn't unusual in this part of the city. Many of the merchants simply didn't have the wherewithal to afford an alarm system, while others couldn't justify the expense because of the response time of the local law enforcement, if, indeed, there even was a measurable response time. Brick waved Dogman into the store ahead of him. The heat washing over them was such an extreme change, that it took both men several seconds to gain orientation and an ability to focus.

At Brick's urging they moved toward the back of the store down an aisle that displayed paper products on one side and condiments on the other. "Get comfortable for awhile," Brick uttered, while removing his cap and gloves. He noticed that Dogman wasn't doing the same and told him to do so and put the items on the floor. Brick imagined that Dogman wasn't as willing to run without them. He motioned for Dogman to back away from his cap and gloves and told him to sit down. The two men just stared at each other.

Brick took the time to study the man. According to Two Spoon, every one supposedly knew this guy. Brick thought he knew just about everyone who mattered but he couldn't place this man's face at all. Dogman's clothing gave the clear indication that he was without residence but there was something about him that seemed out of place. His hair, although choppy, was short and the growth on his face couldn't have been more than four- or five-day's worth. Those two details belied the typical street person's attention to personal appearance. There was also an aura about him that was unlike the others. He seemed to care little about Brick's reputation. Brick didn't seem to instill fear in him and, even now, Dogman held his gaze. Just as surprisingly, he showed concern for others by attempting to move the mother and daughter to safety. Concern for a stranger, particularly when it might bring harm, was not a trademark often exhibited on the streets.

"Why are you helping these people?" Brick queried.

Before Dogman could answer, a door in the back wall of the store fifteen feet from where they sat began to open. As the door slowly swung outward into the store, the twin barrels of a shotgun protruded from the opening. With freakish quickness for a man of his stature, Brick was at the door and wrenching the shotgun from the hands of the startled store owner.

Brick looked hard at the new man and whispered, "We're only here to get warm. Go back upstairs and we'll be gone before you know it."

The man recognized the visitor in his store and seemed to relax while backing away slowly. As he turned and began to ascend the stairs that were now visible through the open door, he spoke loudly but with a comforting tone to whoever was upstairs. Brick did not understand the alien language but knew no call to the police would be made.

When the door closed and he turned around, Dogman was gone. So, too, were the stocking cap and gloves.

On the move again, Robert progressed as covertly as he could, staying close to the buildings, hoping to blend into their darkness, and skirting down alleys and in and out of decaying structures whenever he could. He wasn't overly cold but it was painstaking, nevertheless, because of the snow and wind. The question that Brick had asked just before the shotgun appeared and Robert had bolted through the storeroom and out the back door repeated itself in his mind. Why was he doing it? It wasn't something that he had contemplated at the time. He was just wandering as he always did. Thinking about nothing… thinking about everything… being a silent witness. Walking kept the mind moving, kept the boredom at bay. And the boredom had become deafening as of late.

When he had first hit the streets, the quiet and loneliness were a welcome break from the tempest that had become his life. In his mind, countless times, he had played out everything that had happened over the previous several weeks before Karen had finally left him. There had been so many things to ponder, so many things that had gone wrong, so many things he thought needed solving, that roaming the streets with his mind in high gear made the time pass quickly. That first year had actually gone by quite rapidly. As the first year faded into the second, the thoughts still filled his mind but they had lost their urgency and he began to realize the monotony of them. Somewhere along the line, he had determined that it could not have been different. The economy was what it was and he had put himself into a vulnerable position. Although he should have been able to depend on his business partner to sacrifice his fair share when things turned ugly, as time passed Robert would more frequently understand his partner's decision to just leave. Still, it left a bitter taste in his mouth and, despite sometimes understanding the decision, Robert would go to his grave never waivering in his opinion that Tommy Abernathy had no right to pull out as quickly as he did.

"You're going to Texas? When?"

Tommy Abernathy inhaled deeply. He tried to look Robert in the eye but found it difficult. Ever since he had spoken with his brother three weeks ago, he'd been contemplating this moment. He had underestimated how uncomfortable it would be. "This weekend." It was barely more than a whisper. "My brother wants me to come work with him."

"In his property management business?"

"Yes."

"What about our property management business?" Robert's tone hardened, his anger starting to rise to the surface. He looked his business partner in the eye, although, it might have been mistaken for a glare.

Robert's tone and steady gaze caused Tommy's defenses to heighten. "Robert, what business? Everything's fucking tanking. You know it. Hell, the whole state's tanking. Our occupancy is below fifty percent and every single property is upside down."

"So you're just gonna fuckin' bolt? Leave me hanging?"

"I'm hanging, too. My name's on all those properties and my credit's gonna be worth shit when this is all over. It's better to walk away than pour more money in. Let the banks foreclose."

"Pour more money in? I'm the one that's been pouring the money in. Your money is all tied up, remember?"

The sarcasm of the last statement didn't escape Tommy and his tone matched his partner's. "It is tied up. And it's because of me we got the loans in the first place, remember?"

Robert was temporarily stalled because Tommy's last statement was true. When they had started the business a year and a half ago, Robert had no credit. Screwing around in college, falling short of graduating and a stint in the service made time go by quite quickly. After that, he had moved from mundane job to mundane job while he tried to finish his business degree at night and before he knew it, he was thirty-two years old and hadn't really even started life. Despite how some might judge his lack of forward movement into adulthood, he harbored some diligence and had managed to save sixty-some thousand dollars. When Tommy and he met, their friendship was genuine. They both shared an interest in real estate and felt that it was not only an admirable, manly way to make a living but a sure-fire way to make a lot of money. Property appreciation had been exhibiting a strong head of steam for some time and they wanted in on it. Tommy had the credit worthiness but his money was tight as it was already invested. With little convincing, Robert offered his resources and it was shortly thereafter that their first property was purchased.

Early on it was an easy game. Buy the property with as little down as possible then wait a few months. Refinance the property for as much as thirty to fifty percent more than what it had been purchased for just a few short months before and take the excess and buy more property. Before long they had several properties, both commercial and residential, and Robert's nest egg was diminished to almost nothing. It didn't matter to him, though, despite it being only on paper, his net worth was skyrocketing. Over-priced values made it so.

Unforeseen by many, the state's economy hit the skids. It started with a slow-down in the auto companies, their arrogance finally being rewarded, and was soon followed by company after company moving out of state, their mantra being the cumbersome level of taxes being assessed. The real estate market quickly followed suit. Values dropped because of the uncertain economy and before people could react, although it's uncertain what they could have done anyway, property values more often than not fell below the amount mortgaged. Job loss added to the woes. How could you move to find another job when you couldn't sell your home for as much as you owed? Robert and Tommy found themselves in the same situation as so many others. To add to their burdens, they began to lose tenants, making it necessary to pull money out of their own pockets to satisfy mortgage payments. The remainder of Robert's nest egg disappeared in a flash. Even Tommy had managed to come up with some funds, however meager, to help. For the last few months they failed to make many of their mortgage payments timely and the banks were becoming more vocal in their protests.

Robert's shoulders sank in resignation. "So we just let the properties go back to the banks?"

Tommy saw the numbness in his partner's eyes. He felt sorry for him. Not that his own life was great at the moment, but at least he had a job to go to. And he was creating space between himself and here. "I don't have another answer, man. We don't have any money to keep funding these things and who knows when the market will come back. I'm willing to walk away."

Robert looked at him for a few moments, his mind searching for an answer. He was suppressing his anger, anger that wanted to be heard, but suppression was losing. "That's easy for you to say. You've got a job. You'll still have a steady stream of income. I got nothin'. I've invested all my savings. Why can't you break free some of that money you've got invested to keep us afloat?"

"I can't. And even if I could, it wouldn't make any sense to throw good money after bad."

It was then that Robert realized his partner's selfishness. "Bullshit. You've let me spend my entire savings and, other than a few bucks you've doled out over the last couple of months, you've spent nothing."

"Robert, it is what it is. You're not stupid. Where's this gonna go? You wanna try to make it work, go ahead. Tap Karen's savings and try to hang on. It's gonna be years before prices recover. I'm done. I'm outta here."

The finality of Tommy's statement signaled the end of their partnership. Deep down, Robert knew Tommy was probably right. Still, he couldn't rectify the fact that he had spent all of his savings on this venture while Tommy had come with very little. Whatever Tommy's money was tied up in, it was still safely tied up. Right or wrong, he couldn't stifle the thought that he'd been suckered.

Sometime during the second year the cynicism took hold. He was the victim and everyone that had been a part of his life had turned their back on him. It was then that he needed no one. He pictured himself a drifter and was convinced it was an honorable way to exist. Someone who could live off the land. Friends were needless. Living alone, being alone without the company of others, would prevent one from being a victim. Even now, knowing his mind was not quite right at the time, he felt he had been at his most lucid. He learned the streets, the buildings and houses and the people that lived as he did. But he wanted to do it better. He excitedly welcomed the challenge of finding his next meal or a warm place to stay the night without having the means to procure it. He realized the importance of personal hygiene due to the inaccessibility of doctors and dentists and found ways to wash himself and keep his body hair to a minimum. It was during this time that he finally accepted Yellow as his one and only companion. A companion that would not leave his side and never turn her back on him. They had become one. They had become Dogman.

The cynicism had since abated. Common sense saw to that, as did Einstein. He had tried to shun Einstein but the man was just too interesting, too different from the others he had met. And Einstein would not be shunned. Robert would try to walk away but Einstein would simply follow along, ten feet behind, delivering soliloquy after soliloquy. His elegance was almost hypnotic. Early on from time to time, a question seemingly directed at Robert would sneak into Einstein's discourse and be ignored. Einstein would just continue on as if he expected no answer. When Robert finally warmed to the man, their conversations were intellectual and long. Though unspoken, their friendship was something they both needed. Their lifestyles, however, dictated that the time spent together was limited. Closeness with another was unacceptable. It could lead to revelations. It could give a false sense of dependability. Revealing too much about one's self or growing to rely on another left one open to vulnerability. It was a luxury that was unaffordable in such an existence. Despite these rules, Einstein had made him realize that he was still alive, that he was still a part of the human race. He was being a silent witness, but only to his own life.

It was happenstance that he had been in the alley when Lonnie's vehicle had pulled up in front of the old warehouse. It was a natural attraction to watch what ensued. From the demeanor and actions of the various participants, Robert knew the woman and girl were not there willingly. He knew of Lonnie's reputation. He knew of Gerard's.

He had heard the stories. Had he happened upon this situation a year earlier, he would have walked away. He wasn't the uncaring person now that he was back then. He had recovered a good portion of his compassion. His spartan lifestyle had allowed him to act on instinct. It peeled away all of the notions, all of the excuses, that cause a person to be cautious.

He hadn't thought at all. Hadn't considered how he could actually help the women. He just knew. And he beseeched them before any conscious thought could surface. He didn't regret that act now but he was astounded at the influence Gerard and his men held. He realized now that, in Gerard's and his men's eyes at least, he was a dead man walking but, curiously, that affected him little. His recent lifestyle, as was that of those who lived on the streets with him, was a meager existence and very close to the edge. Not the same edge as those who chose to take chances, but an edge, nevertheless, that was just as close to the line between life and death. The hunger and the needfulness and the loneliness caused the body to break down expeditiously. The me-first mindset of the streets, borne of necessity, begat violence and crime that was only a corner or a shadow away at all times. Death, or at least the thought of it, was never far away. Robert surmised it was simply numbness that suppressed the threat of Gerard. What did concern him was that his actions, which others might perceive as reckless, could be endangering the very people he was trying to help.

He finally arrived at the abandoned Department of Public Works building. He looked to his left and to his right to make certain he was alone before crossing the wide avenue that ran in front. It was deserted. The descending and drifting snow made the traversing of the street more time consuming than was normal, causing him to be out in the open longer than was comfortable. The dying wind that still managed to howl discouraged him from doing anything but trudging directly toward the building, keeping his eyes straight ahead. Had it not taken so long to cross the avenue he might have gone unseen. If he had turned his head to the right to take one last look he might have seen Two Spoon and Lieutenant John Draganchuk enter the street a block away and look in his direction.

CHAPTER THIRTEEN

1:07 a.m. Friday

"Hey, that's him," Two Spoon said excitedly, pointing toward the man making his way across the street.

Draganchuk put his hand on Two Spoon's outstretched arm, pulled it down slowly and with his other hand put a gloved finger to his lips. He tugged on Two Spoon's coat pulling him toward the corner of the building. "We don't want him to see us. Just watch where he goes."

"That's cool."

Nothing about the shadowy figure moving across the street reminded the lieutenant of Robert Huntley. Draganchuk hoped that his new friend didn't snap to the fact that he was already suppose to know where Dogman was holed up. "Are you sure that's him?"

"That's him, sure 'nuf. I knows it."

Despite the lack of recognition, now convinced he was watching Robert, Draganchuk's mind filled with recollections...and questions. He was mesmerized, wondering how this person, dressed as he was, could be his friend. So enraptured was he that Two Spoon was a good thirty feet away by the time Draganchuk noticed his absence.

"Where you going?" he called out.

"I...I'll go find Lonnie. You stay here and make sure Dogman don't leave. When we get back, me and you'll split up that money, man."

Two Spoon was supposed to have led Draganchuk to Lonnie. He hadn't any idea how he was going to deal with Gerard's goon, he was going to cross that bridge when he got to it. But this had worked out even better. Lay out Two Spoon and then no one would know where Robert was. He began moving toward Two Spoon but got no closer. The little man was moving surprisingly fast considering the conditions. Draganchuk reached for his weapon but hesitated. Regardless of the circumstances, shooting a man in the back was not something he could bring himself to do. It contradicted every oath he had ever taken or made, whether in uniform or not. It was ingrained. So he let the man run. His plan would have to be liquid.

The lieutenant made his way toward the Department of Public Works building and entered the same door he had seen Robert go through minutes before. It was only a door he passed through but it was another world that he entered. The thick, hovering smoke assaulted his eyes and throat instantly and both involuntarily spasmed in response. The blinking and coughing made him double over. Perhaps that too was an involuntary response… get lower to the ground to avoid the smoke. Unfortunately, there was no avoiding it. The room was filled with it. He swung around and began to feel his way back to the entrance. Before he exited, his body subconsciously began its shallow breathing and the coughing ceased. Draganchuk turned back toward the room, his eyes nothing more than slits. He could make out three oval shapes of glowing orange thirty feet or so away through the palpable air. He couldn't see anything or anyone near him, and, not that he would normally trust that feeling in these conditions, he did not sense any immediate danger. He stood in his spot by the door for several moments allowing his eyes to adjust to not only the atmosphere but the light as well.

After a time, the stinging in his eyes subsided and he could make out the room in which he was now standing. It appeared to be a large vehicle bay. The ceiling was twenty feet from the floor and the wall to his left consisted of three fifteen-foot wide garage doors. It was quite evidently a place that would allow for housing and maintaining a motor pool for vehicles that were larger than an automobile. At the back, opposite the garage doors, were several more doors of normal size that provided egress to the remainder of the building. Other than the three barrels of burning trash in the middle of the room and the people that huddled around them, the rest of the room was bare. Whether or not the cement floor or the cement block of the walls had ever been painted would remain a mystery.

Draganchuk studied the forms that surrounded each barrel. Some were looking in his direction, some weren't. After several seconds he no longer held their interest. The lieutenant found that curious and continued to gaze at them. He could not imagine how they could ignore him. Wasn't he a stranger who had entered their space without being invited? Could they not tell that he didn't belong here? He watched them awhile longer and couldn't help but feel that they simply just didn't care. A moment later he realized how cold he had been and how inviting the barrels were and began making his way across the room.

He chose one of the barrels and headed toward it. Without any communication, the people warming themselves there squeezed tighter together to make room for him. He removed his gloves, stuffed them in a pocket of his parka and held his hands out over the fire.

While rubbing his hands together he glanced around at the faces that surrounded the barrel. It wasn't easy but he managed to conceal his shock. The hollow cheeks and sunken eyes were horrifying when viewed from a distance of inches. Ashen skin that appeared fragile and almost transparent, seemed stretched taut over the bones of the cheek, chin and forehead. His stomach turned in response to the sight. He caught the gaze of the man directly across from him. A permanent grimace was etched on the man's face, revealing what was left of his teeth. Draganchuk could plainly see four front teeth, one on top and three on the bottom. Half of each tooth that he could see, the half closest to the gum, was very dark. He gave a slight nod to the man but received no acknowledgment in return. As he looked around at the others once more, he could see that they were now looking at him with interest. Not just at his face, but his clothing, as well. His was not tattered. There were no buttons or zippers missing. The elasticized linen at the end of the sleeves of his parka was still intact. Sensing what might be going through their minds, he chose to stare at each one of them intently, boldly, and stand a little straighter. After a few moments, they, too, seemed to sense something about the lieutenant and averted their eyes.

Draganchuk let the warmth move up from his hands, through his arms and into his torso. Not a word was spoken within the groups at any of the barrels. It took Draganchuk awhile to realize that his presence was not the cause of the silence. A knowledge permeated his body and filled him wholly with sadness. Given his chosen vocation, some of this knowledge he already possessed. As with many things in life, when one is able to apply academic knowledge with practical application, the truth becomes clear. These people had nothing to say to each other. He studied the individuals around his barrel and stole glances at those hovering around the other fires. They had been reduced to nothing more than sheep, standing silently in groups, giving their attention to whatever could satisfy their current need. Their lives were so empty that there was nothing worthy of discussion. Staying alive for another day was their only accomplishment. They were so far separated from the outside world that they were not only incapable of discussing current events, they had no interest in them.

At one point, the lieutenant locked eyes with those of a young boy at the next barrel over. He could not tear his eyes away and they stared at each other for several seconds. Draganchuk guessed that the boy could not have been more than nine years old. He couldn't imagine the circumstances that brought the boy to this place. He didn't want to imagine the hopelessness that he could see in his young eyes. The adult standing next to him finally put her hand atop the boy's head and turned it away from the lieutenant. Draganchuk continued to look in the direction of the boy, his sadness deepening at the forsaken child. He shook his head, wondering how this country, so rich in its excesses, could allow a true waif to exist.

His body warm now, he shook off the wretchedness that engulfed him. He focused on the job and considered how to proceed. Something told him that asking those around him where he might find Robert would be a waste of time. He studied the six identical doors at the back of the room without a clue. He moved toward the one furthest to his right, opened it and saw nothing but blackness. The other five revealed the same nothingness. Had it been physically possible at the moment, he would have kicked himself for not packing a flashlight. He couldn't convince himself to go blindly down one of the hallways and get lost in the bowels of the building. Not only was it a matter of opting for the correct door out of six choices, but choosing the right one did not guarantee locating Robert, as he imagined each one only led to a maze of more doors and hallways. Draganchuk decided that staying put was his best option. He would bide his time and see who showed up first, his old friend with the females or the bad guys. Fearing for the health of his lungs and eyes, waiting outside was an even better option, at least until he could no longer stand the cold.

When Dogman entered the room the expectant looks he saw on the faces of both Einstein and Allison vanished instantly. The look on his face made words unnecessary. He gazed at Allison with an apologetic visage but she could only avert her eyes. The weariness brought on by the length and strangeness of the day wore on her heavily. Her entire face seemed to sag under its weight. He resignedly shook his head and then related what had transpired.

Allison, visibly shaken now, struggled to keep her voice even in an attempt not to waken Madison. "How do you know this Brick character won't find us? He knows what direction you were going."

"Allison, I lost him over a half an hour ago and I was taking a very indirect route. I doubt he knows what direction I was going in, let alone, finding this place."

"Bullshit!" she said in a harsh whisper, glancing at her daughter, relieved she was still asleep, huddled close to the dog. "You've been wrong about everything so far. These so-called friends of yours have done nothing but betray you. Instead of getting us to safety, you just lead us deeper into this God forsaken city. We would have been better off with Gerard."

Einstein stole a glance at Dogman, whose head was bowed with his hand deep into his hair. "Allison, I can assure you that you would not be better off with Gerard and his men. Their unsavory reputation is neither a myth nor is it unremarkable. Living in this part of the city for as many years as I have, it is impossible not to have witnessed their ruthlessness first hand. The events that have occurred during your visit only further exhibit their ability to control this part of the city. That measure of control is never earned but taken.

"I can also assure you that Dogman is the person best suited to lead you out of this city unharmed." His voice remained calm, kind even, but took on a parental tone as he once, again, came to the defense of his friend. "While you may be correct that certain of his acquaintances have acted with treachery, he has managed to keep you a step ahead of your pursuers. And the longer this pursuit endures, the better your chances. Time is your ally."

She looked from one man to the other. She felt ashamed at her outburst, knew she should apologize, make up for it in some way but couldn't. She was trapped in a place foreign to her with no way to get free. Her daughter was trying to stay warm huddled next to some candles and a mangy yellow dog, whose last bath was anybody's guess. Frustration made words hard to come by. "What now?" she muttered.

Silence filled the air momentarily. Allison and Einstein glanced toward Dogman in anticipation. His hesitation in answering her question was not comforting to either one of them.

"We wait here until daylight. See if the city snow plows show up in the morning."

The looks exchanged between the two men did not escape Allison. "Why did you two look at each other like that?" When neither one answered right away, she pushed. "Well?"

"This part of the city is not a priority," Dogman finally answered, "We can only hope they'll get here in the morning." He paused for a couple of seconds. "It could be later than that."

"Of course it could," she said sardonically, while forcing a brief, humorless laugh. "How much later?"

"I don't know, Allison. But until the storm stops, until the streets are passable, until there's some sort of transportation available, you're better off here than on the streets. It's difficult to even move out there. In the morning we'll check it out and see what's out there. In the meantime, I suggest we try to get some sleep. I know that sounds impossible and I'm sorry I don't have anything better for you right now. But if we don't get some kind of sleep we're going to be even worse off."

CHAPTER FOURTEEN

2:13 a.m. Friday

The snow had stopped falling thirty minutes ago but Two Spoon couldn't tell. The still gusting wind was making the previously fallen snow swirl, giving the appearance that the blizzard continued. Reality was no longer an issue for Two Spoon. His physical and mental states were weakened beyond safe levels. The extreme cold only augmented the lack of sustenance his body craved, both natural and unnatural. Not knowing where to look for Lonnie or Brick stole his purpose. His pace slowed to a crawl. His embattled senses lost their way and he could no longer recognize his surroundings, which only further confused him as a veteran of these streets. He slid along the brick of the building edging toward the corner. Managing to peer around the corner, he saw three round lights bouncing about and then collapsed into a snow drift.

Lonnie, Brick and Carson approached Two Spoon, their flashlights illuminating the inert body lying in the snow. Lonnie looked over at Carson. "Well, pick his ass up and carry him over to that laundromat."

Brick's pounding brought the decrepit, old woman to the second floor window above the entryway. He put the flashlight to his face and a minute later she toddled to the front door and let them enter.

"We need a glass of water, some coffee and a blanket," Lonnie commanded her.

With barely a glance at any of her visitors, she made her way toward the back of the room past a bank of dryers that one might have guessed were as old as she, except that they weren't. Moments later, she returned with a dull red woolen blanket every bit as tattered as she and a glass of water. Lonnie looked at the blanket disapprovingly but she took no notice of it. She turned and left the room again.

Addressing Carson, again, Lonnie said, "Wrap him in the blanket and start rubbing his arms or something. Try to wake him up."

Carson did so with distaste and the finesse of a man his size.

"Shit, man, take it easy," Brick sputtered, "If he ain't dead already, you're gonna kill 'im."

Much to their surprise, for Two Spoon did, indeed, look dead already, he started to regain consciousness with an unsavory series of snorts and gasps. Two Spoon began babbling incoherently and gathered the blanket around him. The three men just stood there open-mouthed, staring at him for several moments.

Before any of them could act, the old woman reappeared with a steaming mug of coffee. Brick took it and thanked her. She acknowledged the thanks with an almost imperceptible nod of the head. She then retreated knowing that the man's thanks was also a dismissal.

Brick put the water to Two Spoon's mouth and the little man slurped at it greedily. Before long, lucidity began appearing in his eyes. He readjusted the blanket and looked at his surroundings, still disoriented. "Fuck, am I cold. Where am I?"

"Bomarito's Laundromat," answered Lonnie, "Do you know who we are?"

Two Spoon looked up at them as if he hadn't noticed the three men hovering over him before now. He blinked his eyes hard a few times and worked his facial muscles. "Hi Lonnie. Hey Brick." He only glanced at Carson for the briefest of moments. Most everyone in this part of the city was afraid of the man. They were convinced he was demented and holding his gaze could not result in anything good.

"You know anything more than what you told Brick earlier?"

"Is that coffee? Can I have some, man?" Brick handed the mug to him. "Brick, did ya tell Lonnie I came with some good info 'afor?"

"I just said that, didn't I, you stupid…" Lonnie shook his head and hesitated, as if stemming his frustration. He decided to cut the little man a break, afterall, he was dead just a minute ago. "I'm asking if you know anything else."

Two Spoon stared at the floor, trying to gather his senses through the fog still left from the extended exposure to the weather. His eyes brightened when the thought came to him. He cleared his throat to speak, but was overtaken by a coughing spell. When he was through, he hacked up a large amount of mucous and spat it on the floor.

"What are you doin'! You can't do that in here, asshole!" Brick said disgustedly.

"Sorry, man, but I couldn't swallow that shit." He gazed down at the putrid puddle, admiring it and wondering why it was such a big deal. "Anyways, I seen that Dogman guy, again. He was goin' into that building on Western. You know, that big ass building they don't use no more."

"The DPW building?" Lonnie asked.

"What?"

"It says Department of Public Works on it?"

"Yeah, that be it. I guess. It's that big ass building on Western."

"All right, let's move," Lonnie commanded the other two and began moving toward the door.

"Wait," Brick said to Lonnie. He nodded toward Two Spoon. "What about him?"

Lonnie stared at Two Spoon for a moment. He disgusted him, couldn't stand the sight of him, but throwing him back out into the weather would kill him. "Let him stay here until he warms up." Later, he'd figure out a way to screw him out of the reward.

"You heard the man. But you rip these people off or cause any damage or any harm to 'em, you're toast. You understand me?" Brick looked at Two Spoon with menace in his eyes. "I will be back to check. As soon as you're warm, you vacate. Got it?"

"I'm gettin' the reward, right?"

Brick shook his head, wondering if he'd even been heard. "We'll see."

"And clean that crap up off the floor," Lonnie said just before he opened the door.

Discomfort makes the time pass ever so slowly. Lieutenant John Draganchuk couldn't believe that less than three minutes had passed since the last time he checked his watch. There was no way to pass the time easily. He was either outside the Department of Public Works building until the cold began to sting or he was inside until his eyes and lungs hurt. Inside or out, he worried about his health, neither seemingly the better option. He noticed that the people around the barrels changed from time to time but he had no idea why or how. No one ever left by the outside door and, from his vantage point, he couldn't see the six doors at the back of the room. At one point, he was determined to see someone come or go and sat off to the side against the wall. Quite quickly, he fell asleep and awoke with a start. He had been checking his watch so often that he was able to assure himself that no more than a minute had passed and that he had missed nothing. He gave up his quest to determine the comings and goings of the barrel hoverers.

Draganchuk happened to be inside the building and gazing at the three fifty-one a.m. digitally displayed on his watch when the three men appeared. Stomping the snow from their feet and immediately coughing, they drew the attention of everyone in the room. All three men put scarves to their mouths in an attempt to breathe easier and scanned the room. They looked in Draganchuk's direction for a moment, perhaps curious as to why he was off by himself, but lost interest when Brick shook his head at Lonnie.

The lieutenant watched the men walk over to the burning barrels and saw the people there shuffle aside to make room. Assessing the three men, even without being able to see their faces, it was easy for Draganchuk to determine which was the leader. He was neither the tallest nor the shortest but he walked in front of the other two and was the one doing the talking. The shorter man, maybe five ten, was very broad. The third man was just plain big, maybe six-foot four and thick. Draganchuk let out a sigh and muttered an expletive under his breath. Unconsciously, he felt for his weapon under his coat.

Lonnie moved to the second barrel when no one at the first admitted to seeing Dogman or the women enter the building. At the second barrel, a woman excitedly pointed a mittened hand at the second door from the left. She was disappointed when Lonnie and his men turned away from her and headed toward the back of the room. With her hand out, palm up, her gaze followed the men. After a time, she let her hand drop, shrugged off the disappointment, a way of life for her, and turned her attention back to the barrel.

Draganchuk's energy was beginning to rev up. Things were starting. He no longer noticed the haze in the room nor the pain in his eyes and lungs from the smoke. He watched the leader and the shorter man make their way to the door pointed out by the woman and then disappear through it. He was buoyed, actually emboldened, that the third man had been left behind, apparently to act as a lookout.

The lieutenant moved toward the barrels.

CHAPTER FIFTEEN

4:04 a.m. Friday

Draganchuk stood by the burning barrels, once again, loitering idly, allowing Lonnie and Brick some time to separate themselves from Carson. He wanted the space to make sure the big man was alone and, hopefully out of earshot. He didn't want to risk the other two coming back to aide the man left behind. After a time, the lieutenant began shuffling toward Carson.

Standing in the darkness at the back wall, Carson tilted his head slightly with curiosity when he noticed the person moving in his direction. He was used to people avoiding him, preferred it, actually, so he found it interesting that someone would purposely be approaching him. At the same time, he couldn't suppress his hatred for these people. He flicked on his flashlight and shined the beam directly into the face of the lieutenant.

"What do you want?" Carson snarled.

With his hand up to block the light, Draganchuk mumbled toward the big man, "What's goin' on?" He could see that Carson was alert. He had thought about just slowly walking right up to him and catching him off guard. When the flashlight came on and Carson spoke, he knew that wasn't an option. Draganchuk realized now that he would have to distract him with conversation or force him to make the first move.

"None' a yer business. Now turn around and go back to where you come from."

"Naw, c'mon man, tell me what's goin' on," Draganchuk said as he continued edging forward. "Is this 'bout that Dogman fella?"

Carson lowered the beam slightly, hoping the person in front of him would drop his hand. He wanted to get a look at his face. He wasn't used to someone being so brazen with him. "What do you know 'bout it?"

The lieutenant barely moved his hand, still inching forward. "I heard you guys were lookin' for 'im." He was close to striking distance now. "Did ya find 'im back there?"

The big man's curiosity ran out along with his patience. "Look, loser, this ain't none 'a yer business. Now, I told ya once, get outta here before I hurt ya."

"Hurt me? I'm just talkin' to ya," Draganchuk said, feigning surprise and readying himself. "What're ya gonna do to 'im if ya catch 'im?"

"Are you deaf or somethin'. I told ya to get outta here."

Carson was ready to lash out. Draganchuk just had to push it a little more. "C'mon, man. I'm jes askin'. Tell…"

Carson feigned a lunge at the lieutenant. Draganchuk's reaction was almost imperceptible. Instead of reading the reaction as that of a man with experience at violent encounters, Carson mistook it for the dullness of movement so often exhibited by the people he so often abused. He was amused by the lack of movement. This time, he swung his right fist earnestly toward the lieutenant's face.

Knowing the blow was coming, Draganchuk evaded it easily. Before Carson's body stopped turning from the momentum of the punch, the lieutenant slammed the flat of his left foot into the side of the big man's right knee. Carson went down to his knees immediately, grimacing in pain and grabbing at his leg. Wanting to be certain no warning would come from Carson's mouth, Draganchuk drove his right fist into the big man's throat. He pulled his revolver from inside his coat and swung the butt of the handle at the side of Carson's head. Normal men would have crumpled to the ground from the force of the blow to the head but Carson didn't. Draganchuk had tried to deliver the blow with enough force to render him unconscious without killing him but it was an inexact science. When Carson didn't crumble and struggled to reach inside his coat, the lieutenant no longer tried to measure the force and swung with everything he could muster. The man went down this time but Draganchuk quickly straddled him with the weapon raised, ready to strike again. When he didn't move, Draganchuk put his hand to Carson's face and forced open his eyelids to assure himself the man would remain motionless. The lieutenant then bent down, picked up the flashlight dropped by Carson with the first blow and calmly walked back over to the barrels. The hoverers watched him coming and instinctively bunched together as he neared. Once there, Draganchuk simply held the weapon out so all could see it and put his finger to his lips, looking from person to person. Although the gesture was clear enough, the look on his face cemented the intent.

Shortly after 4AM, Madison awoke from her nap. "Momma, I have to go to the bathroom." Her voice was low in an attempt at a whisper but everyone stirred, giving proof of their fitful slumber. Allison looked over at Dogman expectantly.

"There's a place down the hall," Dogman answered in response to her look. "I'll take her."

"How far is it?" Allison asked, failing at masking her never waivering wariness.

"Not far. We'll be back in a couple of minutes."

Allison remained quiet. She glanced over at Einstein, who smiled back gently and gave a small nod from where he lay on the floor. Somehow this disheveled old man gave her a modicum of comfort. At least she guessed he was old; it was difficult to tell through his tattered clothes and unkempt facial hair. Allison weighed going with them, so as not to allow Dogman to be alone with her daughter in this vast tomb of a building but her ingrained manners feared that if she insisted on doing so, she would insult both men. Dogman would presume that she still didn't trust him (she wasn't sure that she did) and Einstein might presume that she didn't want to be left alone with him. As miserable as she felt, as disgusted as she was at this whole situation, she silently chided herself for worrying about offending someone.

"Don't be long," she finally said and promptly chided herself again for uttering such useless words. She had no control over anything.

When the dog realized the little girl was up and moving about, it jumped to its feet and began to follow her, nuzzling at her hand.

"Can she come with us?" Madison asked of Dogman.

"She seems to have taken a liking to you. I doubt she would stand for being left behind."

Once they left the room and had only the flashlight to guide them, Dogman took Madison's hand. Yellow suddenly sprinted off ahead of them.

"Where's she going?" Disappointment was evident in the girl's voice.

"I don't know," he replied, choosing not to tell her that the dog was probably chasing a rodent of some sort. "She just likes to run sometimes."

Lonnie and Brick continued moving down the hallway, lit only by their bobbing and weaving flashlight beams. With the surrounding confines as dark and closed in as they were, it was taking some time for their orientation to kick in. As it did, their forward motion slowly increased. Brick was still lagging, pissing off Lonnie, and the two men whispered snipes at each other. The exchanged insults started shortly after they had first passed through the door when Lonnie's light had settled on a rat scurrying away from them, hugging one of the walls.

Lonnie had smiled sardonically then and said to Brick, "Look."

There had been an audible intake of breath from Brick.

"You gonna be all right?" Lonnie had asked with a sneer.

Brick had shone his flashlight directly into his partner's face, knowing that Lonnie would do the same. The look on Brick's face was hard. "Let's keep movin'," he had warned.

A hundred feet or so in they came upon another passage that led off to the right. Just before they reached the corner, they heard a door open and shut down the new corridor. Both men immediately killed their flashlights. Hands to the walls, they edged to the corner and peered around it. Thirty feet down the hallway, another flashlight appeared, pointing away from the spot where Lonnie and Brick now stood. Two hazy silhouettes, one adult and one child, could be seen walking away from them. Beyond the two dark shapes, further down the corridor, within the conical beam of light, they saw the rump of a somewhat light colored animal running off into the darkness. They could hear the silhouettes talking but could not make out what they were saying.

The two men watched intently until the dark shapes disappeared off to the left another thirty feet down the corridor. They started moving down the hallway and then stopped at the door the two silhouettes had just exited.

"I'm guessing that's the kid we just saw." Lonnie said low, "The mother must be in there. I'll take the kid and this Dogman guy, or whatever the fuck his name is. You go get the mother. Hurt her if you gotta. But don't kill her unless you have to."

Hearing that relieved a good amount of Brick's tension. Killing people wasn't something he liked doing. Not that he hadn't but he tried not to go that far, if at all possible. Those he was charged with dunning or reprimanding were given every chance to avoid it and, usually, they came around just in time. The faces of the four who didn't come around were still vivid in his mind, still burnished on his soul. He had always been uneasy in the dark, but those four faces had changed that feeling from uneasiness to outright fear. He could never shake the feeling that if he spent too much time in darkness those faces would be visiting him. Despite this relief, he remembered the words that Gerard had said to Lonnie.

"I thought Gerard said he wanted 'em dead," he whispered to Lonnie as he reached in his coat for his weapon.

"Let's hold off. Maybe we can still save this situation. Maybe this Dogman guy is the only one who has to die."

CHAPTER SIXTEEN

4:17 a.m. Friday

The lieutenant held Carson's flashlight at shoulder height with his left hand, his weapon in his right. He was well aware of the stupidity of this action. He was putting himself in a position of extreme vulnerability that was in stark contrast to his years of training. Although the flashlight's beam extended many feet down the hallway, there was darkness beyond it. He made a perfect target for one gunman in the shadows. He was a sitting duck for two. He extended his left arm fully to the side hoping there was a chance a sniper might mistake the location of his torso. He made his way down the corridor, stopping every so often, shutting off the flashlight and listening. Most times he heard nothing. Other times he could hear the mournful wail of ancient pipes fighting off the pressure of stale air. When he first saw the corner where Lonnie and Brick had been minutes before, he stopped immediately and shut off the light. In the darkness, he listened intently. Still hearing nothing he edged forward, lightly brushing the wall with his right arm and shoulder for orientation. He reached the corner without the benefit of light and looked to his right down this new hallway. For just the briefest moment he saw a flash of light on the left side of the corridor some sixty feet or so away. He moved forward with the flashlight still off, this time with his left arm and shoulder brushing the wall. He passed the doorway that Brick had just entered. The blackness did not allow him to see it. The cement block and steel door did not allow him to hear anything from inside.

Brick opened the door as quietly as he could manage, which wasn't very quiet at all due to the age of all of the working parts. Despite the noise, he saw no one and heard nothing when he entered the vast room. Off to his left through the floor-to-ceiling chain link, he saw the dim glow given off by the candles coming from beyond the wooden counter. He made his way toward the glow. It wasn't until he opened the fencing door that he heard someone behind the wooden structure say hello. He neglected to respond and moved into the room with his gun in plain sight.

"No," Allison moaned. It was a grief stricken moan, delivered with resignation. It was all she could muster when she saw who it was. Both she and Einstein rose to a sitting position.

"Yeah, I'm afraid so," Brick said with eerie calm, eyeing Einstein and wondering who this new player was, "Don't bother to get up. We're just going to stay here awhile until Lonnie gets back with the kid." Brick took in his surroundings. When he was certain he hadn't missed anything, he turned to Einstein, "Who are you?"

Before Einstein could answer, Allison blurted, "Please don't hurt her! She's just a little girl!"

Brick looked back at her and hesitated a moment before answering. "If that's possible anymore, it'll be up to you," Brick said, shaking his head. Allison was sure she was mistaken, but she could almost convince herself that this saddened the man. "Maybe you shoulda thought about that before you ran. We've been lookin' for you all over the place. And if you ain't noticed, there's a goddamned blizzard outside. Not only that, we ain't heard from your lovin' husband. Fact is, we don't even know where the hell he is."

Allison found it curious that she had not thought about Frank the last few hours. Apparently, she had forgotten that he was the cause of all of this. Where the hell was he now? Why wasn't he coming to their rescue? The weak son of a bitch. At this point, he was just one more man in her life that had disappointed her. How was she supposed to explain this to his daughter? She should be frightened, and she was, but at the moment she was more angry.

"You depended on my husband to get you money? You're as stupid as he is."

"Insulting me ain't gonna help you. If you're as smart as you think you are, you'll just shut up and do as you're told."

Not heeding his advice, Allison continued, "I can get you the money, for crying out loud. Where do you think Frank gets his money? You let my daughter go and I'll get you the goddamn money." She paused, her anger drying up just as quickly as it had arisen. "Please," she pleaded.

"I'm sure certain people will be interested in what you're saying. But I'm not the one you should be talking to. So, for now, just shut up." Brick stared at Allison to make sure she got the message and then added, "Please!" in a mocking tone that matched her plea. When she stayed mute, he turned to Einstein again. "Who are you?"

"I assure you, I am no one of consequence, sir. However, I have been most fortunate to cross paths with this lovely and charming lady. If I may say so, I cannot fathom why anyone would want to do her harm. While she may be wedded to a cad, in no way imaginable does she bear the responsibility for his actions. It would be a most unjust and dishonorable act to punish this fair creature for events over which she has no control."

Einstein took a breath. Brick couldn't help himself. His smile was wide and a small laugh even managed to escape. "Wow," was all he could say.

"Sir, I have heard that you have exhibited fairness in your interactions with the inhabitants in this city of ours. Your reputation is that you dispense reprimand, when necessary, swiftly and without mercy, to be sure. But your reputation is also that of a man who, when circumstances offer mitigation, acts with discernment and restraint. Though many fear you, just as many respect you. Surely, a man of your wisdom can see that any harm that might come to this woman would be a great and tragic miscarriage of justice."

Brick stared at Einstein incredulously, trying to process his words.

While focused on each other, neither man noticed that Allison now held one of the candles. Yelling at Brick just as she threw it, he turned his face into the path of the hurtling flame and the still-liquid scalding wax sloshing around in the small bowl that had held the candle.

Madison peppered Dogman with questions as they made their way down the hallway. If not for the subject matter and the surroundings, anyone listening would have thought it was a normal exchange between an adult and a child.

"Is Yellow coming back soon? How can she see anything?"

"She'll come back soon. She always does. Dogs can see much better in the dark than we can."

Despite it being such an ordinary part of human interaction, Dogman felt odd conversing with the child. It had been so long. He had sometimes wondered over the last several months if he had lost the ability to participate in such a mundane activity. He was grateful that he seemed not to have lost his ability to do so. Plain and simple, it made him feel good. He had to admit to himself that it made him feel a little more human.

When they reached their destination, he aimed the beam across the room. "Now, I'm sorry to say that all we have is that hole in the floor over there," he said ruefully. "I'm going to point the flashlight toward it with my back turned."

He couldn't see the look of disgust on Madison's face but he could hear it in her voice. "Oh, great," she muttered. Dogman smirked in the darkness. "I suppose hoping there's toilet paper would be stupid."

"Actually, there should be some nearby." He peaked over his shoulder and located the roll with the flashlight. "So, there," he added, matching her sarcasm.

After a time, Madison finished up. "Okay, I'm done."

Dogman smiled, but only briefly. Looking into the darkness, away from Madison, and seeing nothing, he still knew something wasn't right. Somehow, he sensed the sound he heard, however soft, directly in front of him wasn't the dog. The last thing he heard before the blackness became even blacker was a whooshing sound closing in on his left ear.

After Dogman crumpled to the floor and his flashlight clattered across the tiles, another flashlight illuminated the young girl's face.

"Hello Madison," the voice behind the new flashlight growled, "Remember me?" The beam moved to position itself below the unnaturally ashen face of Lonnie. Given the surroundings and the situation, it was a sight, purposely contrived by Lonnie, that Madison's young mind couldn't comprehend with anything other than utter fear. The strength and weight of that fear knocked her off her feet.

CHAPTER SEVENTEEN

4:23 a.m. Friday

Lieutenant Draganchuk heard the crack of a blunt object coming into contact with something solid and that something solid hitting the floor. Still hugging the left wall, he picked up his pace, arriving at the entrance to the room just as Lonnie reached Madison. His first sight of this room was the pure terror on the little girl's face as she was looking up at her captor. His heart immediately grew leaden. He flicked on his flashlight and pointed it into Lonnie's face when he turned around.

"Drop your weapon."

Lonnie showed little reaction, which was unsettling to the lieutenant. Lonnie held up his hand to block the light and asked with earnest curiosity, "Who the hell are you?"

"It doesn't matter. Drop your weapon, now," Draganchuk repeated.

"Hmm. Sound like a cop," Lonnie said matter-of-factly. He calmly stuck his flashlight under his arm that held the gun, reached down and picked up the girl by the back of her shirt. He stood behind her, the top of her head at his belt buckle, and put the gun to her head. "I don't think so. Maybe you should put yours down."

When Lonnie had assumed his position behind the girl, the beam of his flashlight had bounced around the room. Out of the corner of his eye, Draganchuk spied the inert body lying on the floor. He assumed it to be his friend. His countenance became steely. "I don't care about the girl," the lieutenant lied, "You can both die here or you can live to see another day." His practiced tone, of course, belied his true feelings. Always try to save the innocents but never put yourself in a position where you will both perish. He wanted with all of his heart for the girl to live, but if he relinquished his weapon, he would never leave the building. And the chances were only slightly better that she would survive.

Lonnie considered the lieutenant's words momentarily. The building was dark except for their flashlights. They were quite a ways from the entrance. The girl would be a distraction. Lonnie concluded that all sorts of possibilities existed. More important, Brick was close by and this guy didn't know it.

"All right," Lonnie said with some amusement, as he set the gun on the floor.

"Kick it over here."

The gun made it about halfway. Draganchuk didn't let his disappointment show.

"Now, the flashlight."

The flashlight's progress was impeded by the gun that lay on the floor between them. The light went out when it collided with the hard metal and clattered off to the side.

Dogman had awoken several seconds earlier and had been listening to the exchange through the fog in his mind. Finally, even after more than two years, he had placed the lieutenant's voice. "Drag? Is that you?" he said groggily.

Draganchuk barely glanced in his friend's direction, not that he would have seen his face. Dogman was outside of the conical beam given off by the flashlight held by the lieutenant and Draganchuk was not about to take his eyes off Lonnie. He was thrilled that his friend was alive. He had a lot of questions that needed answers.

"Yeah, Bobby, it's me."

"What...how..."

"Bobby, don't talk now. We'll talk later. Sweetheart, walk toward me."

In her frightened state, she needed urging. Dogman helped. "Go on Madison. It's okay."

The girl started edging her way across the room. She was about halfway when they heard the unmistakable but muffled report of Brick's weapon. A moment later, they should have heard a steel door down the hallway open and shut and, in fact, did but it was as if it was on a subconscious level. Instead, what they did hear was the feral growl and the frenetic clacking of nails on the hard floor. All eyes turned toward the opening to the hallway. Out of the darkness, Yellow lunged at the lieutenant's arm with teeth bared.

Had her aim been better, or luckier, the hot wax might have gotten into his eyes and done some real damage. The small bowl hit Brick in the chin, the liquid splashing about his left cheek and neck. The candle, its flame extinguished in flight, hit him in the ear, the hot wick leaving only a small smudge on his dark skin. The assault did accomplish most of what Allison had hoped, however, as Brick dropped his gun and flashlight in a delinquent attempt to fend off the object flying at him and wipe the heated wax from his body. Allison took off in the direction of the door beyond the chain link, not thinking of her own safety now but only that of her daughter.

Brick recovered quickly. Ignoring the pain of the hot wax still burning his skin, he searched frantically for his weapon. Einstein had scrambled the ten feet across the floor from where he had been sitting and was just picking it up when Brick's foot came down hard on his right forearm. Einstein, no near a match for the much larger and younger man, let out a painful scream and the gun fell from his hand. Brick retrieved the weapon and turned in the direction of Allison. By this time, she was through the chain link door, though not yet out of the room, but far enough away that Brick couldn't see her through the shadows. He fired a shot high in her direction, the bullet ricocheting off the ceiling and walls of the cement room. His failure to stop her was evidenced a moment later when the steel door opened and then slammed shut.

"Son of a bitch!" he screamed. He started to go after her but stopped quite quickly. He turned back to Einstein. The old man was sitting cross-legged and cradling his right arm, swaying back and forth in response to the pain. Brick walked over, knelt down next to him and put the gun to the side of Einstein's head. The old man tried to lean away from the gun, his eyes twitching in anticipation of the impact.

Brick hesitated. Like most anyone else who came in contact with Einstein, it was hard not to instantly take a liking to him. He'd met many street people over the years and this one seemed like no other. His eloquence aside, even given his current sitting position, he could tell that Einstein carried himself with pride, not falling prey to his circumstances. He wanted to just leave him be. Just tell him to stay here and don't get in the way anymore. Then Einstein spoke.

"Young man, you and I share a history. Our ancestors, our blood, are one in the same. Please, don't do this."

Brick's shoulders slumped in disappointment. He would have rather had Einstein appeal to his sense of decency or compassion, the reputation he had spoken of earlier. Where was that now? Instead, the old man played the race card. He gazed at Einstein a moment later, shook his head with dismay and then struck him with a short but forceful blow across the side of the head.

Allison had forgotten about the short flight of stairs leading up to the room. Just as the door was closing behind her, she stepped out into empty space and plummeted down the two deep risers. Her knees slammed into the hard floor and her momentum forced her forehead into the opposite wall. Momentarily stunned, she heard nothing from down the thirty feet of hallway to her right. Disoriented from the blackness and the blow to her head, she had no way of telling which way to go. She chose wrong. Unable to stand and fighting off the stupor creeping into her head, she crawled down the corridor getting further and further from her daughter. She made the corner that she had passed by when they had first entered the building but she didn't recognize that fact. She turned the corner to her left, crawled another ten feet and stopped. Her knees and head screamed out in pain. The confusing blackness of her surroundings was claustrophobic to the point where she felt she might implode. The desperation was overwhelming and she was completely addled. Her state of mind would allow her to do only one thing. That one thing was to cry out Madison's name and she did so as loudly as she could and then, weeping, collapsed into a fetal position and remained there.

CHAPTER EIGHTEEN

4:32 a.m. Friday

The dog saw her master on the ground and sensed his pain. She saw the girl, her new friend, and sensed her fear. She didn't know the human facing away from her or the object he held in his hand and she concluded that he and the thing he was holding must be responsible. Yellow began running at the man. She instinctively shortened her strides to gain better traction on the slippery floor. When the distance was right, she launched herself. When she reached the lieutenant's arm, she bit down on it hard. She could feel her teeth pierce the nylon of the windbreaker and sink into the soft skin. The warm fluid with the metallic taste filling her mouth was satisfying and inciting. When the man went down to the floor with her, her excitement grew and she continued gnawing and shaking the limb. When she first heard her master yell at her in that negative tone, Yellow was still intent on separating the arm from the man's body. With the second and the third loud protest from her master, she finally let go. Reluctantly.

The gun had flown out of Draganchuk's hand at impact and slid across the floor, glancing off Lonnie's shoe. When the lieutenant hit the floor with the dog still attached to his right arm, the flashlight came out of his left. No one had seen where the gun went because neither of the flashlights were being manned at the time. Lonnie recognized what had happened immediately and began feeling around in the darkness for the weapon.

While Lonnie was searching, Yellow remained vigilant and stood over Draganchuk, a low menacing growl coming from her. Dogman continued speaking to her, trying to get her to relax and back off. The lieutenant was looking around for his weapon and glancing in Lonnie's direction. His somewhat panicky movements kept Yellow on guard and her growl became more menacing. Dogman kept trying to calm her.

Lonnie finally located the gun and blindly fired a shot at the ceiling. The ricochet hit the floor close to Yellow causing her to jump and let out a yelp. She sensed that whatever had hit the floor near her was dangerous and capable of inflicting extreme pain and she bolted out of the room and down the hallway. Remembering that Lonnie's gun had been in the middle of the floor, Dogman scrambled for it but came away with only a flashlight. Where the hell was it? He pointed the beam in the direction of Lonnie in time to see him retrieve the other flashlight. It grew quiet quite quickly when Lonnie focused his light on the two men and pointed the lieutenant's weapon at them.

"Wow. That was exciting," Lonnie said sardonically, "I guess things have changed a little bit, huh?" He walked over to where the lieutenant lay. "So, who the hell are you?"

With great difficulty, Draganchuk tried not to let the pain in his arm steal the even tone of his voice. "Lieutenant Draganchuk, St. Lucille Police Department."

"Huh, no kidding?" Lonnie responded, still seemingly amused by the whole situation. "Kinda thought that might be the case. You're kinda far from home, aren't you, Lieutenant?"

More often than not, police officers got lucky because perps didn't want the murder of a cop on their hands. It caused the courts and the public to lose any compassion they might have had. More importantly, though, it incensed other cops, who would go out of their way and not hesitate to avenge the death of a brother in arms. Lonnie's face was plainly illuminated by the other flashlight and Draganchuk could see his eyes clearly. His face was dull and expressionless but his eyes were intense. There was no mistaking the look of hatred. Draganchuk knew then he wasn't going to be one of the lucky ones. Lonnie fired off two rounds into the lieutenant's chest.

"No!" Dogman cried, anguish spilling out of him, "No! Why? You son of a bitch, why?"

Dogman crawled over to the lieutenant's body and knelt over it. As he stared into Draganchuk's lifeless face, blame and regret overtook him immediately, and totally. It was oppressive, seemingly pressing him to the ground and holding him there. Memories from years past assaulted his mind, creating a rushing sensation in his head that further immobilized him. He knew Draganchuk had come to help him. Despite deserting him and their friendship so many months ago, he had still come. Dogman knew he was responsible for his friend's death. His inner turmoil was urging him to join his friend.

"Get up," Lonnie commanded.

The words broke through Dogman's wall of guilt that hadn't had time to set. The anguish that filled him started to give way to a simmering hostility. As if Lonnie's words had nudged Dogman's anger over the crest of a hill, the momentum of the emotion increased as it charged down the slope. He rose slowly, purposefully, and faced his adversary. Dogman pointed the beam of the flashlight directly into Lonnie's eyes.

Lonnie's eyebrows raised when he read the look on his face. He shook his head and warned, "Don't do it."

Dogman took a step toward him.

"What're you doing? I'm going to kill you. Is that what you want?"

Dogman said nothing. But before anything further happened, a sound from the corner of the room demanded their attention. Both flashlights moved simultaneously, focusing on the spot from where the sound had come. In the confusion of the previous moments, they had forgotten about her. Madison stood there, her face reflecting her struggle between fear and anger. Her lips were turned inward, fighting to stem the tears that dotted her cheeks and the soft whimpers that escaped her mouth. The sight was heartbreaking but made more so by the irony of this eleven-year-old girl, who only hours before had been building a snowman in her suburban backyard, holding Lonnie's gun and pointing it at its owner.

Brick exited the candle lit room just as Lonnie fired the shot at the ceiling. This drew his attention to the right. The dog's yelp and scampering off only cemented his focus in that direction. He couldn't see Allison between himself and the room from which the commotion had arisen and wondered briefly how she could have gotten down the corridor so quickly. He never considered that she might have gone in the opposite direction. Not knowing where Allison was and not knowing what part the animal played in all of this, he made his way cautiously down the hallway.

He was within fifteen feet when the next two shots went off. The first thing he saw when he finally peeked around the corner into the room was the body sprawled on the floor, the right arm and the floor around it stained dark. Craning his neck still further, he could see Lonnie and another man, who's face was hidden, pointing their flashlights at each other. He barely had time to wonder why there was another man in the room and if Dogman was the one standing or the one bleeding on the floor before the flashlights shifted their aim to the corner.

Brick's mouth fell open at the sight. The juxtaposition of this young girl with flowing auburn hair against her two small and delicate hands wrapped around the cold steel of the weapon was mesmerizing. Earlier, in her company, he had tried not to gaze upon her because it sickened him that she had been dragged into this. Seeing her now sickened him even more. He had harmed many people in his life, people he had convinced himself had earned it in some way. There was no way that he could convince himself that this girl was deserving. He was frozen with indecision. He could only watch.

Both men could see Madison's hands trembling. Neither man was thinking the girl had either the wherewithal or the courage to pull the trigger, and neither man thought she would hit her target if she did. Beyond that, their commonality ceased. Lonnie spoke first.

"Young lady, you need to put down that gun."

Dogman's first thought was to go to the girl and take the gun from her young hands. Seeing her holding such a violent and evil thing created an emptiness in his soul. The reality of the situation dictated otherwise. "Madison," Dogman said quietly with a catch in his throat, "this man is going to hurt you and your mom. I know it's hard, honey, but you have to aim the gun at him and pull the trigger." If given the chance, he would severely reprimand himself later for trying to convince an eleven-year-old girl to shoot a man.

"That's my gun, girl, and I know the safety's on. It won't even fire. Do you even know how to work a gun?"

"He's lying, Madison. Don't listen to him. Aim the gun at him and pull the trigger."

Madison's face remained conflicted. The tears started streaming down her cheeks and her lips quivered with confusion. Dogman began inching toward Lonnie. Lonnie was slowly raising his weapon in the direction of Madison. In the darkness, Brick raised his gun and aimed.

From somewhere down the hallway, loud enough for all of them to hear, came Allison's loud and mournful wail of her daughter's name.

A small sound came from Madison's mouth in reaction to her mother's call. As the three men watched her face, the distinct transformation that took place there, the sternness that took over, a sternness that was not that of a young girl, forced their hands. Lonnie was bringing his weapon up quicker now, his eyes growing large. Brick's finger started adding pressure to his trigger. Then another sound came, this time from the floor near Dogman's feet. It caused the slightest hesitation in all three men.

But not the girl.

In the next moment, Madison pulled the trigger. The kick of the weapon knocked her off her feet once again. She and Lonnie hit the floor simultaneously.

When Lonnie disappeared from Brick's line of fire, the girl accomplishing what he had intended, he lowered his weapon and headed quietly but quickly down the hallway. He turned the corner to his left and came upon Allison still lying where she had collapsed. They gazed at each other briefly through the beam of the flashlight. Neither one said a word and Brick never slowed down. When he exited the hallway, he came upon Carson, still in a crumpled pile. He simply stepped over him and exited the building. Then he left Lordmont.

CHAPTER NINETEEN

6:04 a.m. Friday

The three of them and the dog finally exited the old Department of Public Works building shortly after six AM on Friday morning when the yellow snowplow, emblazoned in blue letters with The City of Lordmont on its side, followed by three police cruisers and two EMT vehicles pulled up in front. It was then that Allison allowed herself to relax. She didn't relax when Madison and Dogman found her lying in the hallway. She didn't relax when Dogman used Lonnie's cell phone to call for help. She couldn't even relax during the hour plus wait, even though no one was threatening her and her daughter. The police officers were a most welcome sight. The clean heat inside their patrol cars was only slightly less welcoming.

The sound that had come from the floor near Dogman's feet, the sound that had caused the briefest break in the men's concentration and quite possibly saved the lives of the women and Dogman, had come from Lieutenant John Draganchuk. The sound was the lieutenant finally and audibly inhaling life-giving air. The Kevlar had prevented the two bullets from penetrating the lieutenant's body. It could not prevent the severe contusion that was still forming, nor the fracture of the rib cage beneath. It could not prevent the heart momentarily stopping from the extreme force of the two direct blows.

During their wait for the local authorities, Dogman and the lieutenant had a chance to converse. Influenced by the situation and the injuries both men were nursing, the conversation remained tentative and neither one delved into the deeper issues. When Draganchuk was rolled away by the EMTs, Dogman said to his friend that he was maybe ready to talk about it and indicated, without promising, that he would get in touch.

After a time the technicians had done what they could on the scene for Einstein's concussion and broken arm. As they carried him from the building toward the emergency vehicle, Dogman, Allison and Madison walked alongside the gurney with him. By the time he was situated inside the vehicle, he was fully awake and seemed quite content.

He looked at his friend and said, "Well done, Robert." His voice was weak, his injuries stealing his typical resonance. The use of Robert's real name was not lost on the three. "You have done society a great service by delivering these fair maidens out of harm's way. The only duty that remains is to see them safely home." He reached out his hand toward Robert, who grasped it in his own. "It appears that I shall be indisposed for a few days, so, until then, remain vigilant. I can only hope that you will await my return as eagerly and earnestly as I."

Robert laughed softly. "Of course. You get well, E, and I'll be waiting for you."

Einstein then fixed his eyes on Allison and Madison. "Ladies, I will be forever grateful at having made your acquaintance. While I know it will be most difficult, I beg of you ever so humbly to think of me most kindly as I do you and not associate my existence with those who have been mercifully dispatched." The emergency technicians, who had been temporarily enraptured by Einstein's words, grew impatient. "I must bid you farewell now. I will think of you often with fondness and wish you much bounty in your endeavors."

As the three of them were escorted back to one of the cruisers, Madison looked up at her mother. "I really like him but I never know what he's saying."

The officers had offered to transport all of them to their homes.

Without hesitation, Allison accepted their invitation, while she was pushing her daughter toward the vehicle. The officers looked at Robert, realizing the irony of the question. The discomfort of the silence that followed was growing until Robert laughed and declined the offer.

Allison wasn't sure why she had invited him to the house. Robert wasn't sure why he had accepted. Perhaps, it was simply to avoid the awkwardness growing to epic proportions, as it seemed destined to do when they began to say their goodbyes. Before they knew it, Robert was in the front seat of the patrol car and Allison was in the back with Madison and Yellow heading toward the Lordmont suburb of Birchwood.

He had barely weathered the stares, the questions and the expressions of gratitude from Allison's father and mother. As she shooed her parents out the front door of her home, the reluctance of the couple to leave their daughter alone in her own house with this strange man was plainly written on their faces. Standing alone in the foyer of the Mayweather residence now, Robert knew then that he had made a mistake in coming there. Being on the streets everyday, moving about in abandoned buildings, interacting only with those of similar circumstance, it was easy to forget that he didn't practice the normal customs that human beings perform. In stark contrast to his current surroundings, the raggedness of his clothes, his unkempt hair and the smell emanating from him was suddenly exposed as if he were standing alone on a stage, a powerful spotlight blinding him. His desire to flee was overtaking him.

When Allison noticed that Robert had not followed her into the kitchen, she returned to the foyer to find him simply standing there. Though she didn't know the source of his discomfort, it was evident in his demeanor and she had to coax him into the kitchen. During the trip from Lordmont, she had grown strong in her conviction to invite this man into her home. As she considered the events of the last eighteen hours in the safety of a police cruiser, she was finally able to realize what Robert had done for them. At the very least, she owed the man a hot meal, a hot shower and a night in a warm and comfortable bed.

As it was still morning, she scrambled some eggs, fried some bacon and made toast. While she cooked, he sat at the kitchen table adjacent to an oriel window that looked out on an expansive back yard blanketed in snow. They talked intermittently, while Madison and Yellow ran around the house. Allison felt guilty every time the dog ran by, knowing she wouldn't be able to wait until next Wednesday to have the house cleaned. Though it was not voiced, both Robert and Allison wondered at the girl as she played gleefully with the dog. It wasn't that long ago that she had taken a gun in her hand, pointed it at a man and shot him to death. They both worried about the consequences.

Their conversation throughout breakfast was light, as it generally is with strangers. In Allison's mind, it was also unrewarding because she learned nothing more about him and was at a loss as to how to garner such information. Within thirty minutes of finishing up breakfast, it became obvious that all three of them were beginning to surrender to the lack of sleep from the previous night. Even Yellow had curled up at Madison's feet under the table and hardly stirred when the girl rose from her chair. Allison showed Robert to the guest bedroom with the adjoining bathroom. She laid out towels and a set of Frank's pajamas and said she'd see him that afternoon.

Later that day, sometime in the early afternoon, Robert awoke with a start. His discomfort at his surroundings had not left him. He lay there for a time trying to locate the source of his consternation but it was elusive. The things he experienced in the Mayweather home this day, the food, the shower, the bed, were all things that he remembered clearly, but yet they were still foreign to him. One of his first conclusions was that he was not yet deserving. Or, perhaps, he just wasn't ready. Regardless, it was just as well, knowing where he'd be tomorrow.

He dressed and tiptoed to the second floor to find Yellow. She was in Madison's bedroom sleeping on the end of the bed, her head resting across one of the girl's legs. Yellow lifted her head when Robert peeked in but she didn't move from her spot. He whispered to her to come but she remained where she was. He walked quietly into the room toward the bed but before he got near it, the dog let out a low growl. Robert looked at her curiously for a moment. When he moved toward her again, the growl grew louder. In a whisper that was more like a hiss, Robert told her to come now but the dog didn't move.

"Huh?" he uttered quietly. "Traitor." He watched the dog for another moment and then turned and left the room. He realized then that he was recovering from the trauma that had visited his life before he had hit the streets because he didn't blame the dog one bit.

He made his way through the deep snow in the front yard to the plowed street. He started the long walk toward Lordmont but stopped after a few paces. He turned around and gazed at the Mayweather home contemplatively. His mind swirled with possibilities. They gave over much too quickly to the realities. After a moment, he turned and started walking again.

"I'm going to have to get a new dog."

THE END